Drama High, volume 16
No Mercy

by
L. Divine

Praise for *Drama High*

L. Divine listed as one of the "Great authors for Young Adults."
-JET Magazine

"...Attributes the success of Drama High to its fast pace and to the commercial appeal of the
series' strong-willed heroine, Jayd Jackson."
—*Publisher's Weekly* on the DRAMA HIGH *series*

"Abundant, Juicy drama."
—*Kirkus Reviews* on DRAMA HIGH: HOLIDAZE

"The teen drama is center-court Compton, with enough plots and sub-plots to fill a few episodes of any reality show."
—*Ebony* magazine on DRAMA HIGH: COURTIN' JAYD

"You'll definitely feel for Jayd Jackson, the bold sixteen-year-old Compton, California, junior at the center of keep-it-real Drama High stories."
—*Essence* Magazine on DRAMA HIGH: JAYD'S LEGACY

"Our teens love urban fiction, including L. Divine's Drama High series."
—*School Library Journal* on the DRAMA HIGH *series*

"This book will have you intrigued, and will keep you turning the pages. L. Divine does it again and keeps you wanting to read more and more."
—*Written* Magazine on DRAMA HIGH: COURTIN' JAYD

"Edged with comedy...a provoking street-savvy plot line, Compton native and Drama High author L. Divine writes a fascinating story capturing the voice of young black America."
—*The Cincinnati Herald* on the DRAMA HIGH *series*

"Young love, non-stop drama and a taste of the supernatural, it is sure to please."
—*THE RAWSISTAZ REVIEWERS* on DRAMA HIGH: THE FIGHT

"Through a healthy mix of book smarts, life experiences, and down-to-earth flavor, L. Divine has crafted a well-nuanced coming of age tale for African-American youth."
—*The Atlanta Voice* on DRAMA HIGH: THE FIGHT

"If you grew up on a steady diet of saccharine-*Sweet Valley* novels and think there aren't enough books specifically for African American teens, you're in luck."
—*Prince George's Sentinel* on DRAMA HIGH: THE FIGHT

Other titles in the *Drama High* Series

DEDICATION

To my children, Assata and Ajani. All that I am and do is for you. A big shout-out to Mocha Ochoa, Deborah Taylor, DuEwa Frasier and all of the countless sponsors, librarians, teachers, publicists, and other benefactors who continuously work to bring more Young Adult literature into the marketplace. To Amazon for creating a space where authors can stay in their flow. It's been a long time since I self published my first novel The Fight, and it has been an even longer road. This writing life is not easy, but I assume no path worth having is.

The entire Drama High series is dedicated to you, my readers. Thank you for making life brighter. To you, my #Dramatiholics, #Diviners, #DramaHighSoldiers, #LadyJs, and to all of the other die hard Drama High fans worldwide. In particular, you whose names continuously surface on DramaHigh.com, Facebook, Instagram and Twitter. You inspire me to keep going beyond the tears and the strife and the doubt and the fear. You, who inspire me to keep living my dream. Thank you for loving #JaydsDrama. Keep reading and keep believing in fiction. No one can take your imagination away from you— once you have a new thought it's yours to keep. We can change a negative experience into a positive one, make a loaf of bread into a meal, and take a single word and turn it into a song, novel or script. There's no limitation to our powers—individual or collective—so don't be deterred when defeat knocks at your door. Shake it off and whatever you do, keep it moving. That's the only way to get to where you are destined to be. Most of all, remember to have mercy on yourself. And whatever you do, don't look back.

Acknowledgements

"If you try and fail, make another effort, and still another, until you succeed."
-Napoleon Hill

If I had a nickel for every time a critic made me flinch I'd be the millionaire so many of you assume me to be, but I am not a millionaire. I am, however, doing my absolute best to not only continue this series but to also continue doing what I love, which is essentially the point of it all. As much as I want to say that yes, I do it *all* for the love of my readers and for improving Young Adult literacy, that would be an incomplete statement. Plain and simple, I love this ish! I love living in words. That's why I don't let my critics impede my flow for too long. In my opinion, Drama High is the best of both worlds: Real life fiction with a touch of the supernatural. And again, I write this series because I love what I do...all of it: the teaching, the entertaining, and the writing. Some of you have asked how I deal with the inevitable haters. I try to always be gracious and accept the balance that comes with giving my talent to the marketplace. I give credit where credit is do, take the lesson and keep it moving...period.

So, I say thank you to *all* of you who consistently love me during the ebb and not just the flow—mainly my parents and other family members and friends. Thank you to all of those who have had mercy on my children and me. Thank you to Michael and Ricky Beckwith of the AGAPE International Spiritual Center. Your gifts have made a significant impact on my thoughts and attitude. Thank you for sharing your talents, and for inspiring others from all paths to do the same.

7

THE CREW

Jayd
The voice of the series, Jayd Jackson is a sassy seventeen year old high school senior from Compton, California who comes from a long line of Louisiana conjure women. The only girl in her lineage born with brown eyes and a caul, her grandmother appropriately named her "Jayd", which is also the name her grandmother took on in her days as a Voodoo queen in New Orleans. She lived with her grandparents, four uncles and her cousin, Jay and visited her mother on the weekends until her junior year, when she moved in with her mother permanently. Jayd's in all AP classes at South Bay High—a.k.a. Drama High—as well as the president and founder of the African Student Union, an active member of the Drama Club, and she's also on the Speech and Debate team. Jayd has a tense relationship with her father, who she sees occasionally, and has never-ending drama in her life whether at school or at home.

Mama/Lynn Mae Williams
When Jayd gets in over her head, her grandmother, Mama, a.k.a Queen Jayd, is always there to help. A full-time conjure woman with a long list of both clients and haters, Mama also serves as Jayd's teacher, confidante and protector. With magical green eyes as well as many other tricks up her sleeve, Mama helps Jayd through the seemingly never-ending drama of teenage life.

Mom/Lynn Marie Williams
This sassy thirty-something year old would never be mistaken for a mother of a teenager. But Jayd's mom is definitely all that. And with her fierce green eyes, she keeps the men guessing. Able to talk to Jayd telepathically, Lynn Marie is always there when Jayd needs her, even when they're miles apart.

Esmeralda
Mama's nemesis and Jayd's nightmare, this next-door neighbor is anything but friendly. Esmeralda relocated to Compton from Louisiana around the same time Mama did and has been a thorn in Mama's side ever since. She continuously causes trouble for Mama and Jayd, interfering with Jayd's school life through Misty, Mrs. Bennett and Jeremy's mom. Esmeralda has cold blue eyes with powers of their own, although not nearly as powerful as Mama's.

Misty

The original phrase "frenemies" was coined for this former best friend of Jayd's. Misty has made it her mission to sabotage Jayd any way she can. Now living with Esmeralda, she has the unique advantage of being an original hater from the neighborhood and at school. As a godchild of Mama's nemesis, Misty's own mystical powers have been growing stronger, causing more of problems for Jayd.

Emilio

Since transferring from Venezuela, Emilio's been on Jayd's last nerve. Now a chosen godson of Esmeralda's and her new spiritual partner, Hector, Emilio has teamed up with Misty and aims to make life very difficult for Jayd.

Rah

Rah is Jayd's first love from junior high school who has come back into her life when a mutual friend, Nigel, transfers from Rah's high school (Westingle) to South Bay High. He knows everything about Jayd and has always been her spiritual confidante. Rah lives in Los Angeles but grew up with his grandparents in Compton like Jayd. He loves Jayd fiercely but has a girlfriend who refuses to go away (Trish) and a baby-mama (Sandy) that has it out for Jayd. Rah's a hustler by necessity and a music producer by talent. He takes care of his younger brother, Kamal and holds the house down while his dad is locked-up in Atlanta and his mother strips at a local club.

KJ

KJ's the most popular basketball player on campus and also Jayd's ex-boyfriend and Misty's current boyfriend. Ever since he and Jayd broke up because Jayd refused to have sex with him, he's made it his personal mission to annoy her anyway he can.

Nellie

One of Jayd's best friends, Nellie is the prissy-princess of the crew. She used to date Chance, even if it's Nigel she's really feeling. Nellie made history at South Bay High by becoming the first Black Homecoming princess ever and has let the crown literally go to her head. Always one foot in and one foot out of Jayd's crew, Nellie's obsession with being part of the mean girl's crew may end her true friendships for good if she's not careful.

Mickey
Mickey's the gangster girl of Jayd's small crew. She and Nellie are best
friends but often at odds with one another, mostly because Nellie
secretly wishes she could be more like Mickey. A true hood girl,
Mickey loves being from Compton and her on again/off again man, G, is
a true gangster, solidifying her love for her hood. She has a daughter,
Nickey Shantae, and Jayd's the godmother of this spiritual baby.
Mickey's current boyfriend, Nigel has taken on the responsibility of
being the baby's father even though Mickey was pregnant with Nickey
before they hooked up.

Jeremy
A first for Jayd, Jeremy is her white, half-Jewish on again/off again
boyfriend who also happens to be the most popular cat at South Bay
High. Rich, tall and extremely handsome, Jeremy's witty personality and
good conversation keeps Jayd on her toes and gives Rah a run for his
money—literally.

G/Mickey's Man
Rarely using his birth name, Mickey's original boyfriend is a
troublemaker and hot on Mickey's trail. Always in and out of jail,
Mickey's man is notorious in their hood for being a cold-hearted
gangster and loves to be in control. He also has a thing for Jayd who
can't stand to be anywhere near him.

Nigel
The star-quarterback at South Bay High, Nigel's a friend of Jayd's from
junior high school and also Rah's best friend, making Jayd's world even
smaller. Nigel's the son of a former NBA player who dumped his ex-
girlfriend at Westingle (Tasha) to be with, Mickey. Jayd's caught up in
the mix as both of their friends, but her loyalty lies with Nigel because
she's known him longer and he's always had her back. He knows a little
about her spiritual lineage, but not nearly as much as Rah.

Chase (a.k.a. Chance)
The rich, white hip-hop kid of the crew, Chase is Jayd's drama homie
and Nellie's ex-boyfriend. The fact that he felt for Jayd when she first
arrived at South Bay High creates unwarranted tension between Nellie
and Jayd. Chase recently discovered he's adopted, and that his birth
mother was half-black—a dream come true for Chase.

Cameron
The new queen of the rich mean girl crew, this chick has it bad for Jeremy and will stop at nothing until Jayd's completely out of the picture. Armed with the money and power to make all of her wishes come true, Cameron has major plans to cause Jayd's senior year to be more difficult than need be. But little does she know that Jayd has a few plans of her own and isn't going away so easily.

Keenan
This young brotha is the epitome of an intelligent, athletic, hardworking black man. A football player on scholarship at UCLA and Jayd's new coffee shop buddy, he's quickly winning Jayd over, much to the disliking of her mother and grandmother. Although she tries to avoid it, Jayd's attraction to Keenan is growing stronger and he doesn't seem to mind at all.

Bryan
The youngest of Mama's children and Jayd's favorite uncle, Bryan is a deejay by night and works at the local grocery store during the day. He's also an acquaintance of both Rah and KJ from playing ball around the neighborhood. Bryan often gives Jayd helpful advice about her problems with boys and hating girls. He always has her back, and out of all of her uncles gives her grandparents the least amount of trouble.

Jay
Jay is more like an older brother to Jayd than her cousin. He lives with Mama and Daddy, but his mother (Mama's youngest daughter, Anne) left him when he was a baby and never returned. Jay doesn't know his father and attended Compton High School before receiving his GED this past school year. He and Jayd often cook together and help Mama around the house.

Jayd's Journal

Mama's been in the emergency room with the doctors for a while now. Dr. Whitmore's in there with them as her medical proxy— her personal physician and counsel. I never knew what that word meant until tonight. Daddy didn't put up a fight when he was asked to step outside and Dr. Whitmore was allowed to stay, even if it did look like my grandfather wanted to punch the wall.

Netta and her husband have fallen asleep on one of the couches in the waiting area. Daddy's pacing back and forth, simultaneously wearing out the floor and my nerves. I'm posted up in the hallway near the elevators waiting for the doctors to let my grandmother go home. Mama's fine for now, thank God. But Dr. Whitmore knows Esmeralda better than to believe that she's done being the raging lunatic that she is, and so does Mama. Killing one of Esmeralda's favorite pets won't go by without some sort of dramatic aftermath and we'll be ready for whatever she brings our way.

Even with Mama's injuries, she was quick to tell me to use this time to study my spirit lessons like a good little priestess—her words, not mine. Now I have to memorize one odu a week and give a full essay about what it means to me. Only my grandmother would find a way to make me write more when I also have Mrs. Bennett's Advanced Placement English class to contend with this semester. This week's odu as interpreted by Malauna Karenga, one of Mama's favorite writers, is actually helping to calm my nerves for the time being:

Odu Ogbe Tura

Secret slander, undercover ridicule.

There is no one who turns his back who does not become the subject of slander.

12

This was the teaching of Orunmilla when people were directing slander against him.

He was advised to sacrifice.

He heard and he sacrificed.

He said: Now you may continue your slander, but ridicule cannot remove the sweetness from honey.

It is when you direct slander against me that I become extremely wealthy, that I build houses upon houses, that I bring into being an abundance of children and that I become the possessor of all good things.

So, continue your slander.

For ridicule does not mean that honey will not still be sweet.

I agree: Honey will still be sweet no matter the drama. But like honey to a baby, it can also be lethal and I'm in the mood for revenge. Once I know for sure that Mama's going to make a complete recovery Esmeralda's ass is mine, damn the rest. By the time I'm done with her and her crazy house of horrors I'll have to write a new odu in the spirit book about the one who shut down the neighbor next door. I promise, this will be the last entry I write about Esmeralda except to speak of her in the past tense. Her days of torturing the Williams women are over.

PROLOGUE

"Jayd, please be careful," Maman says, leading the way to the river shore. "You never know what's lying beneath the water's surface."

Women and children dot the sandy bank, washing and playing in the sunset's glow. There are several fishermen in the center of the water, peacefully wading in their boats waiting for the bait to catch dinner.

"Yes, Maman. I will." I lift my skirt above my ankles and step my feet into the cool water.

Maman places her wicker picnic basket on the sand and joins me in the river. "Doesn't it feel good, iyawo? Just being in sweet water causes all of my troubles to disappear." She let's down her jet-black hair and allows it to fall freely to the middle of her back. My mother always comments on how strong the resemblance is between herself and my great-grandmother.

"Yes, it most certainly does." My stomach growls and reminds me of the good food waiting for us inside the basket. "I'll set up for dinner," I say, inhaling deeply and taking in the humid air. I look into the water and catch my reflection in all white before my eyes focus on the sky's mirror image. I then notice huge boulders, fish and other things I can't make out hidden beneath the façade just like Maman said there would be.

I turn around and walk toward the shore, or so I think. My toe slips on a rock I can't see. My eyes now stare at the sky above and the stars that only I can see.

"Jayd!" Maman screams, but her voice fades into the background just like my consciousness.

"Jayd, indeed," a mysterious voice says. I cannot tell if it is male or female, human or other. But it sounds ancient whatever it is.

"Open your eyes!" the voice commands.

14

I obey, calmly allowing the water to move me in the direction of the strange voice. Once my vision adjusts to the darkness, two green eyes appear out of the murky water, and then the rest of the large reptile emerges.

In horror, I attempt to scream and swim away from the beast. My actions are futile. My mouth fills with water; I gasp for air. I'm completely submerged, slowly sinking into the abyss with a crocodile as my only companion. What the hell?

"Calm down, child. If I wanted to eat you my belly would already be full," the crocodile says, smiling. Something about her coquettish eyes tells me I'm speaking to a female. "I have a gift for you, from the river goddess herself." She opens her mouth wide revealing hundreds of sharpened, jade teeth. "These are for you, my dear. They will keep you out of harms way."

I feel myself sinking to the bottom, moving faster the further down I go.

"Go on, take as many as you need. I don't have all day," the crocodile says, moving closer to me.

I look at my options and choose to trust that the reptile is telling the truth. Suddenly, I feel like Hushpuppy in The Beast of the Southern Wild: tired of being scared.

I reach in between the beast's jaws and snatch one green incisor from her gum. A small amount of blood drips onto my hand as the tooth turns into a common river stone, much like the one I slipped on a moment ago.

"You'll need more jade than that to stay alive, iyawo. Keep pulling."

"But it's not green anymore," I say, amazed at the stone's transformation.

15

"Your ashe will restore its power, Jayd," the snaggletooth crocodilian says. She again opens her massive jaws and urges me to keep pulling. "Come on, girl. Maman must be terrified. If you want to make it back to the top you're going to need more stones."

"But that makes no sense. I'll sink if I take too many."

"Jade never fails the object of its protection, my child," she says, sounding more like Mama than a crocodile. "Keep pulling!"

I do as I'm told, snatching out as many teeth as my arms can hold. With every pull I rise closer to the top until I'm finally back inside of my own head.

"Jayd, are you okay?" Maman asks, kneeling down beside me. No one else seems to be aware of my fall.

"Yes, I am," I say, sitting up. I rub the bump on the back of my head, baffled by the experience. I look around and notice the small stones from my vision encircling my body just beneath the water's surface.

Maman catches my gaze and notices the same thing. "Whatever the river goddess gave to you is yours and yours alone. Don't share your vision with anyone, not even me."

I continue staring at the rocks remembering what and where they once were. My head begins to freeze much like when my mother's powers take over my own. As the cold spreads to my forehead the rocks begin to illuminate their original green hue.

"You now possess the power of the river, Jayd," Maman says, her eyes equally aglow. "Whoever's bold enough to cast the first stone in your direction will surely perish under your site."

Last night's dream is still heavy on my mind as I walk down Caldwell Street on my way to work. With Pam's homegoing service and

16

Esmeralda's attack on Mama both occurring last weekend, this seemed like the longest week ever. I'm just glad Mama's finally feeling better. She's not one hundred, but the color's slowly coming back to her cheeks. The medical doctors said she might have contracted rabies from the crow's attack that knocked her out. Against my grandmother's loud objections, they gave her several injections to prevent any further infection. Dr. Whitmore, however, has another theory on what caused Mama to pass out after being pecked by Esmeralda's pet.

Mama's being stubborn and won't stop working for a minute. With Halloween around the corner, her and Netta's clients are anxious to get a hold of their annual protection potions and other good luck charms. I know it's important to keep it moving, but my grandmother needs to sit down somewhere. Mama's too strong-willed to listen to reason from the grown folks in her life and I'm not the young one to make her listen, even if I think I could get her to yield a little. Besides, I've got a lot on my plate and can definitely understand the urgency to get shit done in a timely fashion.

It's hard to be productive when my transportation's on shaky ground. My mom's car has been acting funny all week and I don't know what to do. Rah's usually been my go-to guy for car issues but I'm trying to break him like the bad habit he is. With him and Trish playing big-happy-dysfunctional family for the custody hearing, I need to stay clear of him no matter how many times he calls or texts.

"Hola, Madres," I say, entering Netta's Never Nappy Beauty Shop. Just being in the sweetly scented space makes me feel better. "Sorry I'm late. The little Mazda's being temperamental—again. I didn't want to chance it so I took the bus instead."

17

"I'll have Jeremiah take a look at it if you like," Netta says, loudly clamping the hot curlers before using them on my grandmother's hair. It's unusual for her to do Mama's hair on a Saturday morning, but Mama was still on bed rest for her usual Tuesday appointment. At least they're getting it in before our clients arrive. It's sure to be a very busy day.

"Please Netta," Mama says, turning her head to the right so I can give her a peck on the cheek. "You know your child's no good after work."

"You're right about that, Lynn Mae. But Jayd's family. I'm sure Jeremiah will make time for my favorite godbaby."

I return Netta's hug and smile knowing that I'm her only godchild. "I'd appreciate that very much." I place my purse and jacket inside of my work locker and put on my apron ready to get down to business.

"Have you been studying your odu, iyawo?" Mama asks, reminding me that I need to wash my whites. It's been months since my initiation yet it still feels like it was just yesterday that I devoted my life to my head orisha, Oshune. I may have become a priestess that night but I still feel like a child.

"That's because you are," Mama says, catching my thought. "So, what did you think of the odu?"

"I thought it was lovely," I say, walking toward the back to wash my hands and face before greeting the shrine. "I don't know how sweet I can be when someone's talking smack about me or my family, though."

"I hear that, little Jayd," Netta says. "Especially with the likes of some people."

18

"Some people like Esmeralda?" I ask, stepping back into the main room. Instinctively, I grab the bowl full of dirty combs and brushes ready to clean them.

"That heffa's always at the top of my list." Netta replaces one set of hot curlers back inside of the miniature oven and claims the other. "If I could smack that woman dead in the face I would do it in a heartbeat."

"Don't worry," Mama says, calmly. "We've got something for her, and then some more." Mama's emerald eyes glow with a thought only she possesses. I wish I had half of her spiritual skills.

"Did you find out what Dr. Whitmore thinks caused you to pass out?" I ask, running warm water into the basin.

"No, but I did a reading and figured it out. When that damned bird pecked me it drew blood, Jayd. That's what she was after all along. I just need to fortify myself against whatever evil she's plotting and I'll be fine. Esmeralda's demise is eminent now that we've found her main weakness in those damn animals of hers."

Netta shakes her head and rolls her eyes. She better than anyone knows how stubborn her best friend can be when it comes to her own well-being.

"But I thought you said we can't do anything to the snakes because they're sacred?" I ask, remembering the dreadful discovery after Pam's service last Sunday. Using Queen Califia's sight to garner my mother's vision, I was able to see Emilio and Misty's souls trapped inside of Esmeralda's newest pets.

"We can't, but we can influence her godchildren," Mama says, coolly. "Where there's a will there's most definitely a way, Jayd. And that's where you come in."

Ah hell. Here we go again. I want to stay as far away from Misty's wicked ass as I can, and Emilio always annoys the hell out of me. I say we go Buffy the Vampire Slayer on Esmeralda and Rousseau, fixing her crazy godchildren in the process.

"I heard that," Mama says, looking at me in the mirror's reflection. "Don't even think about going after Esmeralda by yourself, you hear me?"

"Yes, ma'am," I say, disappointed that she caught that thought.

"We'll do things by the spirit book, and my way, of course."

"Listen to your grandmother, Jayd. That heffa's gone off the deep end and is trying to take y'all down with her," Netta says, turning Mama's chair to face me at the washbowls.

"I hear you both loud and clear," I say, rinsing the first set of combs.

I wish Mama couldn't hear me at-will sometimes because what I'm thinking is the exact opposite of what she's telling me to do. I understand that she's the head priestess in charge, but she didn't witness herself bleeding from the head and then passing out. That will never happen again, not on my watch. Whatever work I do on the side has to be kept secret, but I'll be damned if I give Esmeralda and her wicked crew home court advantage again. Both Mama and Netta will be none the wiser as long as I learn to keep my mouth—and my mind—shut.

"As long as I've known you, you've been a lot of things, but stupid isn't one of them. So it begs the question as to why you would think it alright to come through that door and start something you know you can't finish?"
-Mama
Drama High, volume 14: So, So Hood

~ 1 ~
KISS & TELL

It was a long workday but I'm glad Mama's getting back into the swing of things. My plan was to find a couple of different ways to kick Esmeralda's ass, but Keenan surprised me with dinner and a movie at UCLA. The student union is like a miniature city and I loved every minute of it. I even befriended a cool graduate student who happens to be in a wheelchair. Savannah and I immediately hit it off when she came in talking smack to Keenan. She's like an older, spunkier version of me.

"Thanks for the bite," I say as Keenan turns off the engine. "I enjoyed meeting your friends."

"Not a problem at all, my lady. Besides, I'm not done yet." Keenan kisses my right earlobe almost sucking the gold hoop off.

I still get so nervous when he kisses me: It's like the first time every time. I'm loving this new vibe between us, not to mention all of the perks that come with hanging out on a college campus with my new boo. It feels so good that I want to run and tell the world, but I'm still keeping my new romance under wraps, especially around Nigel and the rest of my crew. Their allegiances have always been split between Jeremy and Rah, and adding Keenan to the mix would invite too much drama onto a beautiful thing.

My phone vibrates and halts our make out session just in time. My mom was right: Keenan's energy can be too hot and heavy for me sometimes. He's in college and used to having sex. I don't know how

21

long he'll wait for me but I'm glad he's being patient. I don't know how long I can wait, either.

"What's up, Nigel?"

Keenan, undeterred by the intrusion, continues to nibble on my neck.

"Jayd, I need you to hook me up tonight. UCLA just called and they want to see me tomorrow for some important business."

"Nigel, I'm off tonight, not to mention it's late as hell," I say, trying to stifle my giggle.

Pleased with my response, Keenan moves on to my left my shoulder.

"Jayd, please. I'll pay you triple."

I for one am glad Nigel's allowance has been reinstated now that he's moved back in with his parents. It's doing wonders for my bottom line.

"Fine, Nigel. I'm at my mom's crib. See you soon."

"Aren't you forgetting something?" Keenan says, sucking my shoulder so hard I'm afraid he'll leave another hickey. "We're still on a date, Miss Jackson."

"I know, and I don't want it to end."

"And it doesn't have to," Keenan says, looking into my eyes.

"Duty calls, baby," I say, pecking Keenan on the neck before exiting his Jeep Wrangler. I love this truck. Maybe I can save up enough for my own one day. I can't wait to get off the bus. I haven't missed riding public transportation at all, even if I'm glad to have the option.

"Okay, Jayd. Remember to come up for air after work, preferably with me," Keenan says as I walk up the stairs. He's blocking the driveway but lucky for us no one else is pulling up at the moment.

"I'll text you when I'm done braiding."

"And tell Nigel to stop throwing salt in my game or I'll forget to block him on the football field next fall," Keenan says, winking at me. Something about that last remark doesn't rest well with me.

I stop midway up and turn to face him. "That sounded more like a threat than a message."

"Don't worry, Jayd. I always do my job. You'll see."

My cheeks burn with embarrassment and desire. Keenan makes me feel a way I've never felt before. "Goodnight, Keenan," I say, reaching for my keys.

"Goodnight, Jayd." Comfortable that I've finally reached the front door, Keenan puts his truck in reverse and backs out.

I unlock the multiple bolts on my mom's apartment door and enter the dark living room.

"*Girl, I told you about that boy*," my mom says, invading my thoughts. "*You're playing with fire, messing around with a college football player.*"

"*Mom, I'm not messing around with anybody*," I say, turning on the lamp closest to the front door. I wonder if my neighbor Shawntrese is home from her date yet. We can compare notes later if she is.

"*Life's not a soap opera, Jayd*," my mom says. "*People don't catch sexually transmitted diseases after sleeping around on television. In real life, people catch shit and it may never go away.*"

That reminds me of the KJ and Misty gonorrhea debacle last year. "*That won't happen to me, mom. When and if the time comes you know I'll use protection.*"

"*But it can, even if you both wrap it up. That's why you've got to be careful out here Jayd, especially with those college boys. It's their job to*

23

sleep with as many girls as possible before they graduate."

"Really, mom. No degree or career involved at all, huh?" I say out loud as if she's standing right in front of me.

"*Don't sass your mother, Jayd,*" my mom scolds. "*I may not be there to physically slap you right now, but I'll give that ass a rain check until I come home tomorrow if need be.*"

"No need, mom. My badd." I grab my hair bag out of the hall closet and set up shop in the dining room. I would ask Nigel about Keenan's comment but I don't want to make a big deal about nothing.

"*Good night, Jayd. And heed my words, little girl. I know what I'm talking about.*"

"*Yes ma'am.*" After I'm done braiding Nigel's hair I'll get to work on finding a mind blocking potion or something to keep my two moms from invading my thoughts at-will. I love our gifts of sight and all but the shit's getting to be a bit much.

I can hear Nigel walking up the steps two at a time. If I didn't just talk to him I'd swear he was pissed.

"Hey Nigel," I say, letting him inside. "Ready to get that fro in order?"

"Fo sho, my sister," Nigel says, kissing me on the cheek. "My shit is ratchet right now."

"Yes, it is," I say, touching his tangled hair. "Have you and Mickey made up yet?"

I already know that the answer is no but I'm hoping for the best. After the way he went in on Mickey during our last African Student Union meeting I doubt that they'll get back together, but stranger things have happened.

"Hell no," Nigel says, taking his customary seat at the table. "Did you know that Mickey got that fool out of jail by claiming she was with him on the night of Pam's murder?"

"Yeah, she told me she was thinking about doing it. I told her it was a dumb idea," I say, remembering her revelation on the day of Pam's home going service. "Nigel, Mickey's just scared. She does some of the stupidest things when she lets fear run her imagination."

"It doesn't matter anyway," Nigel says, putting three twenty-dollar bills down on the table. "I'm suing Mickey for custody of Nickey."

"Say what?" I ask, completely shocked.

"My mom and I agreed that it's the best thing to do for the baby," he says, matter-of-factly. "Mickey's, well, Mickey. And G is a thug nigga. My daughter deserves a better life than they could ever give her."

I begin combing through Nigel's hair and hope that Oshune's touch through me will calm his hot head.

"Nigel, you can't be serious. You're not thinking straight."

"The hell I am not. This is the first time I've thought clearly since I met the bitch."

"Okay, hold on a minute," I say, standing in front of Nigel so he can see me. "First you become Mickey's knight in shining armor, now you feel that you need to rescue Nickey from her own mother. What the hell is really going on?" I return to my original post, satisfied with the dramatic eye-opener. "And, how are you going to raise a baby and play college football? It doesn't make any sense."

Nigel tilts his head to the right and allows me to sculpt the first braid.

25

"My mom will have the baby while I'm in school, and I'll be home whenever I can. Besides, I think I'm going to take up UCLA on their offer. That way I'll be close to home and able to see my daughter as often as I want."

"I see," I say, parting the second braid.

Of course Mrs. Esop is in on this idea. Hell, it was probably her brainchild. She sees Nickey as her second chance to raise her perfect protégé and stick it to the girl who almost ruined her precious son's life. Damn, she's good. Every time I think Mrs. Esop's backed off she surprises me by making a bitch move like only she can. I bet Mickey didn't see this shit coming. I told her that providing her ex with a false alibi would come back to bite her in the ass. Her karma came quick, fast and in a hurry.

"Nigel, a year ago you didn't even know Mickey, and now you want to take her daughter away from her because you're angry? What the hell?"

"What the hell is that all hell broke loose in my life when I started dating that girl. My mom's pastor is right; he says that there has to be a deeper meaning to all of it. The only thing I can think of is that I was supposed to be Nickey Shantae's father. Why else would all this shit have gone down the way that it did?" I know he's talking about the fact that Nickey's biological father saved Nigel's life by jumping in front of the bullet Mickey's man shot at him. "I'm done playing games with Mickey. If she wants to be the stupid ass bitch she's become and live her life in danger, then that's her choice. But I'm not letting her do our baby like that. It's not happening, Jayd. Not on my watch."

The brother does have some good points but I can't validate this behavior. "Nigel, I still think you're going about this the wrong way," I

26

say, nearly halfway through his head. "Babies belong with their mamas unless the mother's unfit, which I don't think Mickey truly is."

"That's your opinion, not mine. If my mom's willing to help me raise Nickey then that's exactly what I'm going to do. Mickey can see Nickey whenever she wants to, just not outside of my supervision." Damn, Nigel's serious.

"Nigel, I know that Mickey's not thinking rationally at the moment," I say without revealing Mickey's most recent confessions. "But please be patient with the girl. You knew she was a lot to handle when you first started dealing with her. Don't be surprised now that the same leopard is acting like a cat with spots."

Nigel inhales deeply; I know he's thinking about what I just said. I continue braiding in silence, attempting to weave some peace into his head with every cornrow. Nigel's head nods backwards and I know that he's finally calmed down.

My phone vibrates interrupting our peaceful session. What's Nellie doing calling me, especially this late at night? She's got some nerve. I'm still mad at her for not telling me that she was the one who sent me the picture of Cameron and Jeremy kissing when it first happened.

"Hold up a minute Nigel," I say, reinforcing the comb to maintain the clean part between the last two braids. "Boughetto is calling."

"What the hell kind of name is that?" Nigel asks, not recognizing my nickname for Nellie."

"It's a combination of bougie and ghetto."

"Oh, that's only one chick I know," he says, smiling. "Tell Nellie I said what's up."

27

"Traitors Anonymous. Please state your betrayal," I say, unapologetically.

"And you're the one preaching to me about turning the other cheek," says Nigel, quoting a very popular Bible passage.

I playfully tap him in the head and await Nellie's response.

"Jayd, I didn't know who else to call. I need your help." Nellie's voice is shattered, almost childlike. She's scaring me.

"Nellie, what's wrong?" I ask, glancing at the wall clock. It's almost midnight.

"Can you come get me? I can't talk about it over the phone." What the hell? Before I can tell her off again, she surprises me by doing something I've never heard her do.

"Jayd, please," Nellie begs as she breaks down in tears. "I've got no one else to turn to."

"I'll be right there," I say, picking up the dry erasable marker on the white board attached to the side of the kitchen cabinet. "Where are you?"

Nigel turns his head in concern.

"I'm in the parking lot next to the Crenshaw Christian Center's dome. Jayd, please hurry. I don't feel safe out here by myself."

"What was that all about?" Nigel asks as I hang up my cell.

"Nellie needs us to come and get her. I say us because my mom's car isn't working right now. You mind giving me a ride?"

"I wouldn't have to give you a ride if you'd call your boy back," Nigel says, taking his keys from the dining room table. "You know Rah will hook you up."

"No thank you," I say, grabbing my purse off the coat rack and following Nigel out of the apartment. "My days of calling on Rah are over."

"It's funny how holy people can dish out plenty of advice but never take it."

"Holy people? Really Nigel?" I say, making myself comfortable in the passenger's side of Nigel's classic Impala. "I know of a lot of people who would disagree using that adjective to describe me."

"You're holier than most people I know."

Speaking in holy, I have a sneaky suspicion that Nellie's midnight marauding has something to do with David, her born-again boyfriend. I guess we won't know the truth until we arrive at the scene of the crime.

When Nigel and I reach Nellie, she's disoriented and unusually quiet.

"Something's not right," Nigel says, whispering as if Nellie can't hear us talk because she's sitting in the back seat.

"You can say that again," I say without bothering to lower my voice. "Nellie, what happened? And where's David?"

"Oh, nothing. We just had a fight, that's all."

"What the hell kind of fight did you two have that would cause him to leave you alone on the south side this late at night?" Nigel asks, visibly pissed.

"I needed to freshen up after the revival. I must've been gone longer than I thought," Nellie says, combing through her long weave with her freshly manicured fingernails. "David says I'm too vain as it is."

I know Nellie's not telling us the whole story, but that does explain why she's not wearing a jacket on a chilly night like this. I reach back to wrap my sweater around Nellie and she flinches like she's in pain.

"Nellie, what the hell is wrong with your shoulder?" I ask, looking at Nigel as he glares at a frightened Nellie in his rearview mirror.

"I fell at home," Nellie says, accepting the sweater without the touch. "Nothing major."

Nigel and I exchange glances knowing there's a whole lot more that Nellie's not saying.

"Did that punk hit you, Nellie? If he did I'll rip his ass to shreds," Nigel says, steaming.

"No, no. Nothing like that," Nellie says with fear in her tear-swollen eyes. "I swear it was an accident. David would never do anything to hurt me. He's a sweet guy, and the son of a reverend."

"So are my uncles, and trust me when I say there's more evil in most of them than I've ever seen from anyone else," except from Esmeralda and her folks, but we're not talking about them.

"Just drop it Jayd, okay? Thank you for picking me up but please stay out of this one. I don't need you to save me."

I don't want to save Nellie or anyone else for that matter, but she's my friend and I can't let this go.

"You're welcomed, Nellie." I know Nellie's digging this new dude and she's also feeling guilty for what she did to me, but allowing her to punish herself in an abusive relationship isn't the answer. There are too many red flags about this David character. I'm gonna do a lot more digging to find out all I can about the pastor's son.

"Never piss off a woman who has more designer bags than Mariah Carey."
-Jayd
Drama High, volume 15: Street Soldiers

~ 2 ~
OFF WITH HER HEAD!

"Ouch!" I say, flinching in pain. Ain't nothing like a hot comb searing my skin to make me jump out of my seat.

"Is it too hot for you?" the hairdresser says with a cunning smile. Did she try to press my ear on purpose?

"No, but it is too hot for my skin," I say, reclaiming the chair.

"I'm sorry about that, Madame James. Here, this will help," the young lady says, taking some of the hair cream on the counter and rubbing it on my wound.

I stare at Mama's young reflection in the mirror and admire the hairdresser's work. She's good: almost as good as me, but I rarely—if ever—burn my clients.

"Thank you. It feels much better now." I move my head first to the left and then the right, checking her handiwork. "Rule number one when styling someone's hair: Always make sure they hold their ears down," I say, removing the cape from around my neck. "It's not the client's responsibility to remember, but rather the stylist's not to forget."

"Oui, Madame," the young stylist says, bowing her head in shame.

"When someone sits in your chair you want him or her to feel comfortable and to trust you implicitly. Otherwise, you risk losing your client and quite possibly your livelihood."

I turn the swivel chair away from the mirror. "Please pass me the hand mirror."

Mama's apprentice takes the brass hand mirror from its hook on the side of her station and passes it to me.

"Desiree, you sure do have skills when it comes to those curling irons. Looks like you've been watching me very closely."

"Queen Jayd, you have no idea." Desiree stares at Mama's reflection in the mirror and traps my grandmother in her seat with her vision. Desiree's eyes begin to swirl like crystal blue tornadoes, her hands open wide beside her directing the wind in her powerful glare. Her hair turns gray and begins to whirl around her head like a clouded halo; her long curls morph into snakes right before my eyes.

"Desiree, what the hell do you think you're doing?" I ask, my grandmother's green eyes taking on a glow of their own. I continue staring at Desiree's wild reflection through the hand mirror still unable to move a muscle.

"I'm doing exactly what you taught me to do, Queen Jayd."

The force in Desiree's eyes moves into the center of the wall mirror causing everything in the small shop to shake violently. She moves her hands above her head in the shape of a crown, creates a semicircle and then directs the ball of energy at Mama's hand mirror.

"All hail the Queen!" Desiree says, opening her hands wide.

Mama's green eyes are technically working but I'm still paralyzed, unable to fight back. The shaking worsens and I can't hold on to the mirror any longer. The heavy brass casing smacks me in the forehead and breaks my skin wide open.

"Shit!" I scream, feeling the blood trickle down my cheek.

"That's it, Lynn Mae," Desiree says, sounding more like Esmeralda than herself. "Let the blood of the Queen flow freely. There's power in the Queen's blood." The snakes on her head elongate and stretch out toward my face. All I can do is watch as they fight each other for the red droplets leaving my grandmother's body.

32

"You won't get away with this, Desiree!" I say, doing my best to focus my grandmother's sight on stopping the reptiles but it's no use. "Whatever you're trying to do won't work."

"Are you sure about that, Queen Jayd? After all, it was written that I'd never get this far, and look at us now," Desiree says, putting her head beside my grandmother's, now a part of the reflection I see in the small mirror. "A little bit more of your blood and people might think we're actually twins."

"No matter how hard you try, Desiree, you'll never be a Williams woman."

Mamas green eyes become powerful cyclones of their own and lock Desiree's vision in the mirror as well. Both visions become too much for the hand mirror; it falls to the floor and shatters upon impact.

"No!" Desiree shrieks in pain. "My head! My head!"

I fall to my knees thankful that I can move again, but not for long. I bring my hands to my face and feel nothing but wetness.

"Oh my God," I whisper, noticing Desiree's head writhing about on the floor like a deflating balloon.

I catch my own reflection in the shards of broken glass; I'm covered in blood from head to toe. Everywhere there is skin I am bleeding. My fingers cloaked in red crystals form permanent lines on my face. I cover my throat with my left hand in an attempt to stop the flow but it is too late.

"Too late, indeed," Desiree says, beheading her own reflection in the largest piece of the shattered wall mirror. "We are twins in death, Queen Jayd!" Desiree's headless body comes crashing down beside me.

I stare into the reflective pieces surrounding me and watch helplessly as my grandmother's crown falls to the floor.

"My head!" I scream. I grab my throat and quickly touch all parts of my face and neck to make sure everything's still attached. What the hell was that all about?

After my crazy dream I decided to chance driving my mom's ride and check on Mama before school. I felt like I needed a hug from my grandmother but she's nowhere to be found. I'm pretty sure her head's still on her shoulders, but after everything's that happened around here lately I'd be more comfortable laying eyes on her myself just to be sure.

"Good morning, little Jayd," Esmeralda says with her loyal canine man coming outside behind her. "How's Lynn Mae feeling?"

"You know damn well how my grandmother's feeling, Esmeralda," I say, walking across the front yard toward her house.

"Well, I sure do hope the Queen is feeling better. The last time I saw her she looked a little pale, didn't she, Rousseau?" Esmeralda says to her mate, her crystal blue eyes shining brightly in the morning sun.

"Don't you worry about my grandmother," I say, disarming my mother's car alarm. Netta's son rigged it a bit to get me around for the time being but said that I'd need to invest some cash to get it done right. "She's just fine."

"Are you sure about that, little queen?" Esmeralda asks, her two remaining pet crows flying from their cages and landing on her shoulders. There's something about the way she's questioning my grandmother's well being that sends a chill down my spine. Where is Mama?

"And I'm sorry about how my pets reacted to their home being burglarized, but you do know how strong the trespassing laws are in Los Angeles County," Esmeralda says, petting the evil birds. "It seems they possess the souls of police officers who know how to serve justice when we need be."

No doubt she's got a few officers on her payroll. That would explain how she's able to manipulate the drug game on this side of Compton without getting caught. I wonder if the officers knew part of their cut would come at the cost of their souls.

"Burglarized?" I say. "It was more like an attempt to save kidnapped souls, or have you forgotten about Misty and Emilio's trapped spirits inside of your new snake pets?"

"Oh don't worry about them, mi petite," Rousseau says, stepping in front of his woman. "Our new houseguests are being treated like gods, and fed like them, too." Rousseau looks past me toward the back gate where Lexi walks out, growling at the diabolic duo that turned her against Mama.

"Lexi, no!" I scream, worried for Mama's dog. Ever since she attacked Mama Lexi's been hell-bent on making it up to her owner. "Stay girl; stay!"

"No, let the little bitch come on over," Rousseau says, showing his fangs off with a growl of his own.

"The signs are posted," Esmeralda says, pointing to the red and white squares propped up in her kitchen window. "There's one on the back door too, just in case."

"We already warned you about trespassing on our property," Rousseau says, whistling at Lexi who's ready to attack.

"Our property?" I repeat. "Do you know how many men have laid in that same bed you're trying to claim as yours? And you're barely human or have you forgotten? How the hell are you going to own property?"

35

"There's more than one way to stake your claim in this world," Rousseau says, calming down. I see he's still enough of a man to have his ego checked.

"Be careful, little girl. You don't want to get in over your head, speaking about grown woman shit when you're as fresh as a newborn baby," Esmeralda says, sniffing the air. "Back in the day girls who overstepped their boundaries were swiftly put in their place." Esmeralda brings her right index finger to her left ear and slowly moves it across her throat to the other side.

"If you lay a hand on my grandmother's head or any other part of her I will kill you, Esmeralda. Believe that," I say, hearing Esmeralda's psychic threat loud and clear.

"I think I just heard a threat, Rousseau. Did you?"

"Yes I did, and so did your pets," he says, resuming his pit bull status.

Lexi charges across the front yard before I can stop her. If she dies it'll be on my head.

"Lexi, stop!" I shout, but it's no use. Lexi's already at the driveway split between my grandparent's property and Esmeralda's.

"Tell your grandmother we said hello," Esmeralda says, retreating back inside and taking her animal farm with her. As she closes the door Esmeralda looks down at the growling canine and smiles.

Lexi quiets her attack and replaces her threats with moans of pain.

"Stop it, Esmeralda!" I scream. "What are you doing to Mama's dog?" I run over to Lexi who's now squirming on the ground.

Without another word Esmeralda disappears behind her front door and takes the last bit of my patience with her.

Thank God I wasn't late for school after my exciting morning. I made sure Lexi was okay before leaving but without Mama's eyes to look over her, I'm not sure if she's all good. As if I didn't already have enough drama going on, I unexpectedly started my period. Damn, what a day.

I keep a back-up tampon in my purse at all times, but of course it broke. I really need to clean out this purse or get a bigger one.

"Hola, Jayd," Maggie says, stepping into the bathroom. The bell for third period just rang making me officially late to English class.

"Maggie, what up, girl?"

"Nothing much," Maggie says, hugging me. "Just trying to make it through the day, you know?"

"Yeah, I know," I say, tossing the broken contraption into the trash. They took the tampon machines out of the girls' bathrooms last year forcing us to make the trek to the nurse's office for emergency supplies. Mrs. Bennett better not say a word to me when I walk in late. Pass or no pass, she can choose to be a real bitch anytime she wants.

"I can't wait until Homecoming, Jayd," Maggie says, primping her stiff bangs in the mirror. How does she get out of class at the very beginning? None of my teachers on the Advanced Placement track would ever allow me to miss the first five minutes to use the restroom.

"I'm glad you're excited, Maggie," I say, feeling my cramps begin. "You wouldn't happen to have a tampon on you, would you? Mother nature decided to make a surprise appearance this morning."

"Si, mami," Maggie says, reaching into her purse and pulling out one of the miniature tampons I've always dreaded using. A beaded necklace falls to the floor as she hands it to me.

37

"That looks familiar," I say, smiling at her.

Maggie brings the multicolored eleke to her forehead and then kisses it, just like Mama taught me to do with mine.

"Yes, I thought it would," Maggie says as I claim a stall. "I've always wanted to know more about your religion."

"And I always thought your entire crew was Catholic for the most part."

"We are Catolicos in public, but Santeras at home. My cousins are both very involved in the church and also hold bembes every weekend in Long Beach. You should come sometime."

"I think I will," I say, exiting the stall to wash my hands. "I've never been to any religious celebrations outside of our house."

"It's a date then, yes? I will let you know about the next one," Maggie says, leading the way out.

"Bet." I turn the opposite direction down the main hall. When I reach my class Mrs. Bennett's well into our morning assignment.

"Miss Jackson, so nice of you to join us," Mrs. Bennett says, giving me her full attention.

I drop my backpack down next to my desk in the front of the room and take a seat. I should've asked for an Advil while Maggie was feeling charitable. I feel like I'm going to die in about two seconds.

"You can place your hall pass on my desk. I've already taken roll," Mrs. Bennett says. "Like I was saying before we were so rudely interrupted, I will post the lessons and any supporting documents on my Facebook page. The school's site will also have a link to my page. I've created the page specifically for AP students so please don't share it with your friends."

"That's what's up," Damon, one of her favorite ass kissers says, making Alia smile. I thought her smiles were only for Chase these days.

"That's a very good idea, Mrs. B," Reid says, nodding in agreement. "Highly efficient."

"Exactly my goal," Mrs. Bennett says, proud of herself. "Please read the sonnet on page twenty and then construct an expository paragraph on the main topic. You have ten minutes."

Is there something wrong with me, because everyone else seems to love Mrs. Bennett? Maybe it's just me, but she's one of the evilest teachers I've ever had the displeasure of encountering.

"Miss Jackson, where's your note?" Mrs. Bennett asks, sitting down behind her desk.

"I was in the restroom. That's why I'm late," I say, praying she'll cut me some slack.

"That's all fine and well, Miss Jackson, but without a late pass I cannot let you into this room. Surely you know the rules: No restroom passes during the first five minutes of class do to the pertinent information you've just missed."

"The office doesn't give passes to the restroom last I checked," I say, defensively. Even her diabolical self has to have compassion for a girl with cramps.

"Is the student now the teacher, Miss Jackson?" Mrs. Bennett says, rising from her desk unsympathetically. "Do you think I, of all, people don't know how this school works?"

The other nineteen students try to focus on their reading while Mrs. Bennett continues to make an example out of me, as usual.

"No, Mrs. Bennett. But I have no reason to lie to you. I had an emergency that couldn't wait another five minutes." I don't want to spell it out for her but I will if she keeps on pushing.

"Of course you wouldn't lie to me, because you've been so forthcoming with me in the past, right?" Mrs. Bennett asks, referring to a couple of things I'm sure, but they're all beside the point, especially when I know she's one of Esmeralda's godchildren in a round about sort of way.

"I'm not lying," I say, sick of her bullying. "I was in the restroom and I have the cramps to prove it."

The already silent room is focused on Mrs. Bennett's next move. I think I'm the only student in all of her classes who refuses to back down from her bull.

"You need a pass to enter my classroom late, Miss Jackson," Mrs. Bennett says, reclaiming her seat. "Otherwise, it's an automatic detention referral. Your choice."

Damn it. Why is she messing with me when I'm in pain?

The students look at me and then back to our teacher who's not budging.

"Fine," I say, slowly rising from my seat end exiting the room. I wish I had it in me not to come back, just go to the beach like Jeremy or Chase would do without a second thought. I only know of one place to go when I need a remedy to all school related ailments.

"Ms. Toni, I hate to bother you," I say, entering her office inside of the main hall. When I get all the way inside I see that she's already preoccupied with another visitor. Mr. Cho, the one man who knows his way around this entire campus with access to every room, is the supervising janitor and has worked at South Bay High for over thirty years.

"Jayd, what a lovely surprise," Ms. Toni says, ushering me to

40

come inside. "You know Mr. Cho."

"Of course," I say, reaching out my right hand. "Good morning, sir."

"Good morning to you, too, Jayd," Mr. Cho says, in a soft Chinese accent. I've only heard him speak a few times. He takes my hand and slightly bows his head. "I've heard a lot about you."

"I hope it's all good," I say, forcing a smile. "I wish I could stay and chat but I actually need a favor." I walk over to my school mom and hug her. I have faith that one day she won't smell like the cigarettes she smokes. I gave her a little something for that but it hasn't kicked in yet. Maybe she needs another dose.

"What's up?" Ms. Toni asks, touching the beautiful vase full of exotic flowers on her desk.

Mr. Cho also pays special attention to the bouquet. If I didn't know better I'd say that I just broke up a make out session.

"It's that time of the month and I was late to Mrs. Bennett's class because of it. Sorry to blurt out all of my business, Mr. Cho, but I'm in a bit of a rush." Even though I'm out of the room because of Mrs. Bennett's request, I know she's still going to hold me accountable for the morning work.

"Oh Jayd," Ms. Toni says, hugging me back. "You've got to stay out of that woman's way."

"Me?" I say, near tears. "She's the one who's always messing with me. I don't know what I did to her to make her hate me so much."

"She can't break you, Jayd. That's why most people on power trips abuse those who refuse to bow," Mr. Cho says, kissing Ms. Toni on the cheek. "I've seen Mrs. Bennett break many students, but never one like you."

41

"John's right, Jayd," Ms. Toni says, calling Mr. Cho by his first name. Now I'm really uncomfortable. "As long as she doesn't break your spirit you'll be fine."

Ms. Toni reaches into her desks and takes out her student passes. As the ASB advisor she's got every pass available.

"You wouldn't happen to have any Advil would you?" I ask. What I really need is a heating pad and some of Mama's raspberry tea, but modern medicine will have to do in this moment.

"You know I've got my baby," Ms. Toni says, pulling a bottle out of the first aid kit on the wall and handing it to me. "As long as I'm here that woman won't get away with too much. Success is the best revenge, Jayd. Remember that."

I don't know about that one. I can think of many other ways to get revenge on Mrs. Bennett, and my diploma has nothing to do with any of them. Turning the other cheek with her has run its course. Along with Esmeralda and Rousseau, Mrs. Bennett's on my short list of hating elders that need to be taught a lesson in chilling out on my ass. They only have themselves to blame when I come after them with all I've got.

"Most people would rather see you cry than smile."
-Mama
Drama High, volume 15: Street Soldiers

~ 3 ~
NEVER NOT BROKEN

It was rough getting through the rest of third and fourth period, but it was worth it to finally get to lunch. Chase treated me and Alia to take out and bought dessert. We're so close that my play brother can even tell when I need a good dose of chocolate ganache cheesecake from The Cheesecake Factory, my favorite local restaurant.

"Greetings, scavengers," Matt says, interrupting our feast. It's unusual for the drama club devotee to socialize during lunch even if he and Chase hang out from time to time. He's usually off campus smoking a cigarette somewhere.

"Matt," I say, too busy licking my fork to say much.

"We're announcing auditions for the Fall Festival," he says, passing out the fliers. "It'll be interesting to see who tries out this year."

"You know I'm in," Chase says, reading the neon colored paper—no doubt Seth's contribution. If it weren't for Seth's organizational skills and Matt's physical labor, the drama club wouldn't be nearly as successful as it is. What's Seth going to do next year when Matt graduates with the rest of us seniors?

"Alice in Wonderland," I say, feeling a personal relationship already developing between me and the main character. "Count me in, too." I recall last year's fiasco when Laura thought she was going to steal my part. I dare her and Mrs. Bennett to try that shit again this year. I'll have both their heads on platters.

43

"What's up with your girl, Nellie? She's not looking so good," Matt says, noticing Nellie's passive demeanor.

Chase looks worried, much to Alia's disliking but she can't really say much the way she was cheesing it up for dude in class this morning.

"She had a rough weekend," I say, leaving out the pertinent details of Operation: Rescue Nellie. It's Nellie's story to tell, not mine. And she'll tell whomever she pleases whatever she pleases, whenever she pleases.

"I'm going to see what's up with her," Chase says, letting go of his current girlfriend to check on his ex.

I would walk over there but when Nellie left my mom's apartment yesterday morning she made it clear that she never wanted to mention Saturday night again. Nigel was still asleep on the living room floor when Nellie and I had a brief but telling conversation about her very emotional relationship with David. I think she's in over her head with the preacher's son but she says she can handle it.

"Is it just me or is Nellie good at playing the victim?" Alia says, observing the body language between the two former lovers, both of them my friends. Alia's a cool homegirl but I know where my true loyalties lie.

"I don't think she's playing," I say, further pissing Alia off. Normally I'd be right there with her in thinking that Nellie was up to something—I know she senses the change.

"She says she's fine but I don't know," Chase says, putting his arm around a resistant Alia. "Something's not right."

"Well, why don't you take her home and grill her about whatever's going on," Alia says, sarcastically.

I think this is the first time that I've ever heard the girl use anything but a nice tone with her man. It's funny how jealousy can turn even the sweetest chick into a monster.

"Babe, you good?" Chase asks, finally noticing Alia's foul disposition.

"Yup, just peachy," Alia says, removing his arm and walking off toward the main hall.

"What did I miss?" Chase asks, completely oblivious. Most boys are clueless when it comes to the games of love.

"A lot," I say, smiling at my best guy friend.

Chase looks from Nellie to Alia and shakes his head, finally figuring it out for himself.

I can't be mad at him, but if he were my man I would probably feel the same way Alia does right now. Chase has been hung up on Nellie for two years. That shit doesn't just fade away because he's got a new girl by his side.

"Come on, Chase. We'd better get to Speech and Debate." I'm looking forward to Mr. Adewale's daily topic. He always picks some good ones.

"But seriously, what did I do wrong? Am I not supposed to check on Nellie because we broke up?" Chase asks as we join the procession to fifth period.

"Depends on the chick you're dating," I say, eyeing Alia eye us. "And apparently Alia has a well-hidden jealous streak."

"You're her friend," Chase says. "Did you know she'd trip on me like this?"

"First of all, Alia and I are acquaintances. Don't go throwing the word friend around so loosely," I say, taking my seat. "Second of all,

45

I've never witnessed her on the dating scene before so no, I didn't know she'd trip on you like this."

"Damn, and I thought she was cool like that," Chase says, quoting one of our favorite old school rap songs.

"She was cool like that until you knocked her boots from here to Tijuana," Nigel says, smacking his boy on the back and joining the conversation.

"How did you know what we were talking about?" I ask, accepting the kiss on the cheek.

"I didn't," Nigel says, sitting next to me and putting me in the middle. "It just seemed relevant."

"Damn straight," Chase says, nodding as Mickey and the rest of the class enters the room. "You know what's up."

"Don't we all," I say, glad I'm still a virgin. The shit that happens when sex and love mix is not what I want to deal with right now. So far, none of the relationships I've witnessed end on a positive note once sex enters the equation.

"Good afternoon, class," Mr. A says, calming us down. "Today's topic is global warming. Who wants to take the pro?"

"I will," Emilio says, displaying a big ass smile. What's he so damned happy about? He and Misty don't have full possession of their own souls but seem to be just fine with that.

"I'll take the con," I say before Mr. A can ask. I want to get inside of Emilio's head and see if he knows he's under Esmeralda's spell.

Misty, Shae and KJ look at Emilio and smile, ready for the showdown. Ever since he and I faced off in the race for African Student Union president last year there's been a constant rivalry between my vice president and myself, chauvinistic pig.

"Okay then, Miss Jackson," Mr. Adewale says, writing our names down on the whiteboard. "Remember to site what you can from last weeks' readings to support your opinion. Facts are important even in a mock debate."

"Got it, Mr. A," Emilio says, kissing up to his unwilling mentor. He and Emilio were pretty tight when he first transferred from Venezuela last year, but Mr. A quickly peeped Emilio's crazy card and so did I.

"Get her, baby," Misty says. Baby? They must be official now, and from the heated expression on KJ's face, I'm not the only one just hearing the news.

"There will be no getting of any babies in here this afternoon," Mr. Adewale says, shutting Misty down. I don't know how he maintains his patient composure when hoodrats test him on a daily basis.

Between Nigel and Mickey's fight during our ASU meeting last week and Misty constantly showing her ass, I would've went off a long time ago.

"Emilio, pro has the floor."

Emilio begins his speech defending pro global warming restrictions and legislation. I agree with the premise of the argument, however, I can say I don't think we have much control over nature. The bottom line is that whether I drive a Prius or not, the Earth will eventually do what it does.

"And in conclusion, if we do not adhere to the restrictions that nature continues to warn us about the impacts on our lives and future generations will not only be devastating, it will also be the very end of life as we know it."

"That's what I'm talking about," Misty says, clapping loudly. What the hell?

"Seriously, Misty?" KJ says, pointing at Emilio. "You picked this punk ass know-it-all over another chance with me?"

His boys laugh in the background causing Misty's blue eyes to glow. I guess I'm still the only one who notices the supernatural changes going on with my nemesis.

"Okay you two, pipe down," Mr. Adewale says, tapping his hand on the desk in front of him. "Jayd, con has the floor."

"The Earth is always changing, always broken and there's absolutely nothing wrong about that," I say, recalling one of Mama's wisdom lessons from the spirit book. She wrote about the power of nature when she was about my age, having lived through several serious storms in Louisiana. "She doesn't need us to fix her. She needs us to fix ourselves."

"Church, preach!" Chase says, causing a slight uproar of laughter.

Laura and Reid are not impressed, mostly because Reid knows that I'll take him on any day when it comes to debate, the race for Homecoming queen, and anything else he wants to bring to the table.

"Mr. Carmichael, thank you for the enthusiasm but please hold your comments until the end." Mr. Adewale nods his head for me to continue.

"We're always in motion, and the Earth is always shedding its skin if you will. Volcanoes have always erupted, the ground has always shaken; rivers have always risen only to fall, and brush fires have always burned. The only difference is the recorded human recollection of all of these events."

"Yeah, that's right," KJ says, siding with me just to spite Misty, and from the way she's staring me down I'd say it's working.

48

Mr. Adewale cuts KJ the side eye, his hazel eyes taking on a sparkle of their own. KJ gets the message and allows me to finish my argument.

"Pompeii, the end of the Dinosaur Age and The Ice Age are just a few examples of our collective story. Now, with our so-called advanced scientific technology we think we should be able to predict how the story should end with us at the center. Haven't we learned our lesson yet? Our only option is to play within nature's rules and to literally go with the flow. If the planet is telling us to slow down, then let's do that. If she says it's time to change our excessive lifestyles, then we should consider that. But please don't tell me that she needs our help because you're way off. If anything, we need to beg mother Earth for her sympathy because she holds the power to wipe us clean, not the other way around."

"Say what!" Chase says, standing in applause. "Can the church say amen?"

"Amen!" Nigel says, fanning his silly ass friend. I love them both too much to be mad.

"Well said, both of you," Mr. Adewale says, writing our next assignment on the board. "Thank you, Emilio and Jayd for that spirited argument. Okay class, I need for everyone to give me a page on either side of the subject. Once you're done, switch papers with your neighbor and check it for accuracy."

"Good shit, Miss Jackson," Chase says softly while pinching my right cheek like I'm five years old. "I think my mom will be very impressed with your oratory skills."

49

"Hey, don't be talking about my girl's oratory skills like that," Nigel says, jokingly. "She's a lady." It sounds like my boy's been watching too much Martin on Netflix.

"Y'all are both so, so stupid," I say, taking out my notebook and turning to the section for fifth period.

"Miss Jackson, a word please."

"Yes, Mr. A," I say, approaching his desk.

"I want you to consider entering the first speech competition of the year," he says, handing me a flier with the information.

"Oh, I don't know, Mr. A," I say, reading the requirements. "And it's in West LA on a school night. You know my grandmother's not having that."

"You're grandmother, my godmother, knows I have your best interest at heart." Mr. Adewale takes the paper from my hand and announces the event to the class. "Jayd's just signed up for this event. Any other takers?"

"I'll do it," Emilio says, enthusiastically raising his hand.

Misty looks at her new beau like a proud wifey. Once I figure out exactly how Esmeralda used her magical manipulation to marry their souls I can undo this bull. I wonder if Emilio and Misty realize that their newfound infatuation isn't real. Just a few weeks ago KJ and Misty were hot and heavy, even after her wicked metamorphosis.

KJ's made his confusion well known and isn't taking the trade lying down. KJ rolls his eyes at his ex and Misty returns the hate. They're almost as silly as Nigel and Mickey, who are pretending not to notice one another in the intimate setting, which is probably for the best.

"What the hell. I'm always up for a challenge," Reid says, Laura beaming like the proud first that lady she is. I can totally see them governing some conservative state in the not-so-distant future. That's all she wants to do is be his wife, and all he wants to do is run the world.

"Excellent," Mr. Adewale says, pointing to the board. "All interested persons can sign up after class. A word of advice: Get involved in the moment and not the movement, people. I'm urging you to research recent issues surrounding your topics thoroughly. A lot can change in two weeks."

Bored of the particulars, the rest of the class returns to their work.

"You'll thank me later, Jayd, " Mr. Adewale says, keeping me at his desk a minute longer. "It'll look very good on your college applications. By the way, have you written your personal essay and the requests for your reference letters yet?"

All of a sudden I feel the pressure of more work closing in on me. Will I ever be done writing and reading and filling out shit?

"I have plenty of time for that," I say, also tiring of his speech. "It's only October and most of them aren't due until December at the earliest."

"Jayd, I don't mean to sound pushy but you need to jump on it, iyawo," Mr. Adewale says, one of the only people at school who knows my spiritual status. I still can't believe he was a part of my initiation ceremony, or that I kissed him when I suffered a temporary meltdown. He's a very forgiving brotha.

"I know you're right, Mr. A. Consider me on all of it," I say, returning to my seat. I need to get on my game in more ways than one and today's events have been the motivation I needed to make it happen.

"Are we sharing a vision walk again?" I ask Mama who looks different from what I've ever seen her look like before. Her body looks broken like a puzzle but it's pieced altogether, and she's riding an alligator like it's a horse.

"I don't know, chile. You tell me," Mama says, gripping the wide reptile with her thighs, pulling the reigns tight. "But I know I'm liking this ride." Mama looks more like my mom's age than her fifty-plus years.

"I can see that," I say, admiring her skills at handling the beast. "Aren't you afraid he's going to, I don't know, eat you?" Dream or not, I'd never be as cool as she is riding an alligator. Maybe I've seen too many Discovery Channel specials, but there's no way I'm getting close to that thing.

"Sometimes you have to face your fears in order to do your best work. Victory is right on the other side of struggle." Mama's green eyes grow big as the alligator jumps into the lake, rapidly spinning her but Mama holds on tight. Unable to shake her loose, the alligator plunges deeper into the water.

"Let go of my grandmother!" I scream, leaping into the water. When I open my eyes the foggy water is brightly lit encasing me inside a light-filled cocoon.

My grandmother emerges from the depths of the lake piece by piece: first her fingertips, then her arms, head and the remaining parts of her body.

"Mama!" I scream, terrified of my grandmother being killed. But miraculously she is alive and better than ever.

"I'm fine, Jayd," she says, putting the pieces back together. "This is the natural order of things, just like the Hindu goddess, Akhilandishvari."

"Akhilandishvari," I repeat: I like the way that sounds.

52

"Yes. Her name means 'never not broken'. She is the goddess of always being broken. Sometimes in order to heal we have to first be broken, but never broke down like Esmeralda's attempting to do to you and I, Jayd. Don't let that heffa get to you or Lexi again."

How did Mama know about Esmeralda's bitch contribution this morning? I wasn't even thinking about it.

"I heard your thoughts just now, Jayd," Mama says, answering my unspoken question as usual. "Your subconscious mind is always at work whether you're aware of it or not."

A bright green light shines through the cracks indicating the places where Mama was once broken. "You have to not only face your fears but ride them like a alligator," Mama says. "You have too many people on your side who want to help you succeed, Jayd. Esmeralda, her godchildren and the rest of her lineage have nothing on us. Get over your fears and get to work!"

I shoot up in bed hearing Mama loud and clear. Petty shit has no space in my life. My only concern should be eliminating my enemies one at a time, starting with Esmeralda.

"You need to learn how to balance both of your worlds. That way you'll never be out of your element."
-Mama
Drama High, volume 2: Second Chance

~ 4 ~
CLEAN START

It was difficult getting back to sleep last night after the dream I had of Mama riding a damned alligator of all things. It was the third one this week and they're really starting to bother my sleep pattern. I was so tired after my last client left yesterday evening that I didn't even get to sweep up the hair let alone put away all of my tools. My mother's car is parked in front of the apartment and I know I'm about to catch hell for leaving her place a mess.

"Jayd, what have I told you about leaving evidence of your work everywhere?" my mom says, sifting through her mountain of mail on the dining room table. "This can't keep going on forever, Miss Jackson."

"Mom, I'm sorry, but please don't call me that," I say, plopping down on the unmade couch from my sleep last night. "You sound just like Mrs. Bennett."

"Ugh," my mom says, shuddering at the thought. "I hope I don't need to make a special appearance again on your behalf. It's becoming an annual event."

Before my mom came to South Bay for a meeting with Mrs. Bennett, Ms. Toni and the administration last year she'd only been up to the school once before. Neither she nor Mama wants to venture to Redondo Beach any more than absolutely necessary.

"At least it's my last year in high school. Soon, Mrs. Bennett will be a thing of the past," I say, removing my sandals after a long day and week. I'm so glad that it's Friday I almost want to cancel the two clients I

54

have lined up this evening and veg out. Keenan's going to stop by after I'm done working. I hope I can stay awake long enough to catch up with him.

"Girl, please," my mom says, slitting her green eyes at me. "There will always be another Mrs. Bennett around. Life's full of them, so you might as well get used to that fact."

"I guess," I say, too tired to argue.

"Ain't no guessing about it, girl," my mom says, grabbing her overnight bag and stacking it full of clean laundry from the basket on the floor. "Bitches are everywhere, and apparently they shed." My mom kicks a ball of hair under the table and looks at me like she wants to cuss me out but holds her tongue.

"I know, mom. I'm on it," I say, rising from my makeshift bed and making my way to the kitchen. I take the broom and dustpan from the pantry and get to it.

"You remind me so much of my favorite Aunt DeeDee, your great aunt. I loved the way she did my hair," my mom says, running her fingers through her long, jet-black tresses. "DeeDee actually braided my hair the last night of her life. I didn't take those braids out for eight weeks after her murder."

"Mom, that's a bit much, don't you think?" I move on to the kitchen floor. My last client shed worse than a cat on a hot day. Folks around here really need to start using my products on the regular and not just when I do their hair. It would make it easier for me the next time around but no, they'd rather get whatever products they can from the dollar store and let me deal with the aftermath.

"Not really, Jayd. Think about some of your clients who only want you touching their heads. It was like that with DeeDee. Your braids

55

actually remind me a lot of hers, and she used to make a mess of her kitchen, too."

"Mom, what do you want me to do?" I feel bad about not keeping up my end of our agreement lately but between work, spirit duties and school a sistah is beyond exhausted. "It's not like I can rent a space of my own. I'm only seventeen."

"I'm glad you asked," my mom says, showing me a text on her cell. "I spoke to Shakir this afternoon and he said for you to drop by when you can. He has a business proposition for you."

"Mom, I can't work at Simply Wholesome again, Netta's shop, and maintain my own hustle. I'm getting more tired just thinking about it."

"I know that, Jayd, but just hear the brother out," my mom says, placing the Louis Vuitton duffle bag on her shoulder. "I can drop you off now if you like."

"Wow, mom. Really?" I ask, replacing the broom and dustpan in the closet and checking the clock. I have about an hour before my first client for the evening shows up.

"Yes Jayd," my mom says, retrieving her purse from the coat rack. "Otherwise, I'm going to have to evict you and I don't want to do that to my own daughter."

I know she's joking but not really. My mom can be one cold sistah when she wants to be.

"How am I going to get back home?" I ask, also grabbing my purse. I dropped the car off at Netta's shop so that her son could continue working on it. "The car won't be ready until tomorrow afternoon."

"How did you get here in the first place?"

"I got you, mom." My mom's not the person to go to for sympathy, but she does handle business like only she can—hook ups and all.

When I finally make it to Slauson Avenue the parking lot is packed with Mercedes Benzes, Range Rovers and Jaguars, including Shakir's black Jag parked in front of the restaurant. The long line stretches out of the front door forcing me to enter through the grocery store on the other side of the building.

"Jayd!" Sarah, my former coworker screams. She comes from behind the register to hug me, damn the customers.

"It's good to see you, too," I say, returning the love. I have missed this place, but not Marty, the bitch of a manager who's still on the payroll I see. "Where's Alonzo?"

"He's holding down the juice bar, as usual." Sarah points toward the restaurant entrance where there's a live reggae band playing outside on the patio.

"There she is," Shakir says, stepping into the market from the office space in the back used for storage. "Lynn Marie said you might stop by."

"I really didn't have much of a choice," I say, hugging him. "She told me you might have a business proposition for me, but I have to warn you that I'm very busy these days."

"Aren't you always?" Shakir says, handing Sarah a receipt book.

"Brother Mohammed, this is for you," a young, Muslim brother says, handing Shakir a medium-sized pink box, most likely containing a bean pie.

"Thank you, my brother," Shakir says, handing the man five dollars.

57

"Mohammed, Shahid, Shakir," I say, following him to an empty table in the dining area. "Why so many names?"

I've made the mistake of calling him both Shakir and Shahid, confusing many customers and myself in the process. Rah went through a similar name change back in junior high, wanting everyone to call him Seven because he read some book about black men being God and seven was God's number or something like that. Either way it didn't stick. The name Rah's different enough for most people without adding a number onto it.

"My given name is Rodrick James Armstrong," he says. That name doesn't suit him at all. "My chosen name is Shahid Shakir Abdul Mohammed El."

"Wow," I say, taking a small slice of the pie he's offered. "That's a mouthful."

Shakir laughs at my surprise. "Don't you have more than one name, Jayd?"

He's got a good point there. My spiritual name is Osunlade and my nickname is Lyttle. I guess we all need split identities if for no other reason than to identify people by how they call us.

"So, about that business proposal," I say. "I don't mean to be rude but I've got two clients this evening."

"That's precisely what I wanted to talk to you about," Shakir says, removing his rasta cap and revealing a head full of untamed locks. "I need my locks tightened. Also, Summer's going back to school for business management and she needs an unofficial apprentice to help out with her natural hair business."

"I'd love to take you on as a client but I don't know about working here again," I say, looking at Marty behind the counter. She better not fix her lips to say shit to me, not even hello.

"Look Jayd, Lynn Marie told me that you're hustling hard out of her apartment and it's getting on both your nerves." It's not really bothering me but I guess my mom has truly had enough if she's telling her high school homie about it. "Wouldn't it be better to work out of the back of Simply Wholesome?"

"Isn't there some type of law against a minor doing hair without a license?" I ask. Netta and Mama only allow me to wash clients' heads, never braid or even blow dry for that matter.

"Like I said, you'll be an apprentice. I'll even pay for your cosmetology license as long as you work here. And no, there's no law against you doing natural hair styles, as long as there's no chemicals or heavy heat involved," Shakir says, passing me an envelope.

"*Jayd, take him up on his offer,*" my mom says, making her thoughts well known.

"Your business is booming, Jayd, and it's a really good investment from where I'm sitting. Take a look at the proposal and let me know what you think. And make it soon, please. I really need you to take care of this before it gets out of control," Shakir says, replacing his cap and getting back to work.

I open the envelope with the contract inside and seriously consider his generous offer. My client list will improve, and it's not too far away from Inglewood that I'd lose my current customers. Besides, it wouldn't be so bad getting out of my mom's apartment, not only because of the ever-present smell of cooking hair in the space, but also because the water and electric bill will be less. And I'll be able to save up for another car hopefully sooner than later.

"*Girl, you better make it happen*," my mom says, invading my private thought process yet again. "*I know it's a lot to think about, but we have to work something out. Besides, you know Shakir's a good businessman and who knows, this could be just the opportunity you need to push your own business to the next level. Like you said, this is your last year of high school. Time to think bigger, baby.*"

"*I got you, mom.*"

Even my mom knows that I'll have to talk it over with Mama tomorrow before I make any decisions. Until then, it's back to work for this little entrepreneur.

"You've got to promise me you won't be one of his groupies, Jayd. All the
young brotha needs is controversy."
-Ms. Toni
Drama High, volume 3: Jayd's Legacy

~ 5 ~
WITCH DOCTOR

I finally caught up with Mama who's been working with Dr. Whitmore for the past few days. Rather than meeting Netta and Mama at the shop per our usual busy Saturday schedule, they want me to come to Dr. Whitmore's office before we open. I'm anxious to see what Dr. Whitmore has to say about Mama's recovery process even if I'm missing the extra two hours of sleep I could be getting instead.

"Jayd, close the door!" Netta screams, scaring the shit out of me. The sun isn't up good yet and it's equally dark inside the quaint shop.

"What's going on?" I ask, my eyes adjusting to the darkness. There are three figures; two standing on either side of the one in the middle, who I think is Mama.

"Your grandmother's sleepwalking," Dr. Whitmore says in a low, steady voice. "And we can't wake her."

"Get off of my grandbaby!" Mama shouts, sweeping the broom in the air and nearly hitting her best friend.

"What happened to her?" I ask, completely shocked. I've never seen Mama in this state before. "Mama doesn't sleep walk; that's my Achilles' heel." I don't do it as often as I used to when I was younger, but whenever I do sleepwalk it's always bad news.

"Exactly," Dr. Whitmore says. I can feel his eyes focus intently on mine without seeing them. "You're going to have to go inside of her dream and wake her up."

"How am I supposed to do that?"

61

Before Dr. Whitmore can answer, Mama drops her broom, grabs my face and forces our foreheads together.

"Ahhhh!" I scream out in pain. The surge of our sights hits me like a tidal wave. It's a cold, overwhelming rush, much like the brain freeze I experience when my mom's sight takes over but magnified to the thousandth degree.

"Jayd!" Netta screams, desperately. "Lynn Mae, you have to wake up!" She attempts to free me from my grandmother's grasp but her efforts are futile. Mama's in another realm and possesses the strength of a gladiator.

"Let her go, you spiteful wench!" Mama says, circling the ring with her opponent a few steps in front of her.

"Never!" Esmeralda says, also circling the dirt sphere. "An eye for an eye, a child for a child. Isn't that what the good book says?"

"Depends on which good book you read." Mama twirls her brass sword in the air. That thing must weigh twice as much as any sword I've ever seen.

They both appear to be about twenty years younger. Mama already looks young for her age, but Esmeralda's youthful transformation is a recent manifestation. However, in this vision they both possess the physiques of female body builders.

"Jayd, you have to wake her up," Dr. Whitmore says, adding a calm voice to the mix. "It's imperative that you both escape the vision immediately."

"Mama, it's me and I'm okay," I say, stepping into the center of the cipher. "No one has me."

"Jayd, no!" Mama screams, pointing the sword at me. "Get out of here! You don't know what you're doing!"

62

"Haven't I already told you to stay out of grown women's business, little girl," Esmeralda says, moving closer to me. "I warned you, Lynn Mae. The crown is too big for this child's head."

"Stay away from Jayd, Esmeralda. Come after me if you want revenge."

"Why would I go for old blood when I can have new?" Esmeralda licks the tip of her silver sword.

"You've been after us for decades and you'll never get to her, not unless you get past me first, which will never happen." Mama swings her blade at Esmeralda's head, nearly slicing it off.

"Never say never, Queen Jayd." Esmeralda blocks the attack and counters with one of her own.

Feeling helpless, I bend down and grab a fistful of dirt, and fling it into Esmeralda's cold blue eyes.

"You stupid little witch!" Esmeralda screams, attempting to brush the dirt from her face.

"Mama, we've got to get out of here!" I run over toward my grandmother, pull her arm and attempt to shake her out of it.

"No, Jayd. Esmeralda's using voodoo dolls to manipulate her followers, and she's coming after you next."

"Voodoo dolls?" I ask, remembering Mama telling me about them a while back but we don't work with them—ever. "I thought you said they didn't work unless you believed in them?"

"I never said that exactly," Mama says, watching Esmeralda swing in vain. Without her sight she's helpless. "If the right person makes the right doll anything is possible."

"Jayd, snap out of it," Netta says, shaking me by my shoulders.

"What the hell was that?" I ask, coming to. I notice Mama also waking up.

"That was Esmeralda's handiwork," Netta says, tending to her best friend. "That evil wench is forcing her victims into a walking sleep and then switching their souls with her loyal pets. She's making living zombies out of them, manipulating others to do her dirty work, and she's getting away with it. That's what happened to your friend's boyfriend."

"And happening to dozens of other victims," Dr. Whitmore says, placing several acupuncture pins into a brown, female cloth doll with green crystals for eyes.

Mama rubs the spots where the pins puncture the doll, eventually lying down on the massage table in the center of the room. "I feel like I haven't slept in days," Mama says, groggily.

"That's because you haven't, Lynn Mae," Dr, Whitmore says, placing the doll at the top of my grandmother's head. He begins prepping Mama for an acupuncture treatment of her own. "What's the last dream you remember having?"

"I was riding an alligator, and Jayd was there," Mama says, dozing off. "It was exhilarating."

"That was days ago," I say, holding her hand. "And it was also my dream."

Mama looks at me confused, almost as if she doesn't recognize me. We dream every night without fail and always remember our dreams. Some are just simple REM episodes while others are spiritual messages. When we don't dream it's tantamount to insomnia.

"You're going to be okay," I say, kissing Mama's forehead. I look up at Dr. Whitmore and read the concern all over his usually stoic face. He looks frightened for his old friend.

Once Mama's needles are in place she fades off into a restful sleep. Netta and Dr. Whitmore close the curtain dividing the space in half and pull me into the adjacent room.

"Your grandmother's under Esmeralda's spell," Dr. Whitmore says, solemnly. "The only way to keep her safe and healthy is to keep her in a deep sleep, only waking her once a day just long enough for her to check in."

"No offense, doc but that sounds a little off to me," Netta says, reading my mind. "How will she eat and do all of the other things we need to do to survive?"

"She'll be fine, trust me," Dr. Whitmore says, taking a large book similar to our spirit book off of one of the dozens of shelves lining the walls. "This isn't the first time we've been through this." Dr. Whitmore turns the yellowing pages and stops on one entry in particular.

"This is the largest journal I've ever seen," I say, eyeing the neat handwriting. Every letter and number is precisely written making for a completely legible text, unlike our spirit book. The women in my family have notoriously indecipherable handwriting.

"I already called Ogunlabi to come and help," Dr. Whitmore says, referring to Mr. Adewale by his spiritual name. "He'll be outside momentarily to keep an eye out for any of Esmeralda's watch dogs that may come sniffing around, including Rousseau."

Just the mention of the evil shape shifter's name makes my stomach turn. I wish Lexi could take a bite out of his ass, but I have a feeling that would be the end of Lexi.

"How can I help?" Netta asks, checking out the page for herself. "How to wake a living zombie," she reads aloud.

65

Dr. Whitmore puts his hand over the page, indicating to Netta that it's not for her to read.

"Netta, you can be the best friend you always are. And Jayd, you have to do what you were born to do, young queen," Dr. Whitmore says, sounding a lot like Shakir. "You have to invade Lynn Mae's dreams and beat Esmeralda at her own game."

"Oh, is that all?" I say, shaking my head in disbelief. I can't jump into my grandmother's thoughts at will. She has the illest powers I've ever seen; able to borrow anyone's site and use it however she desires. She can also catch other people's thoughts. I can work my way into other people's dreams but I never thought to try it on Mama.

We reenter the space where Mama's soundly resting, a welcomed reprieve from her active sleepwalking.

"Make sure she understands what's going on," Dr. Whitmore continues, ignoring my sarcasm. "Otherwise she can get lost in that world and leave this reality forever."

"You make it sound like she'll go crazy if she stays asleep too long," I say, scared for my grandmother. I knew there was more to Esmeralda's favorite pet pecking Mama's head than I could see at the time. If I get my hands on another one of her damned birds I'll be eating crow for dinner.

"She will loose her mind, and all sense of time and space right along with it. Most people call it dementia or schizophrenia," Netta says, taking a hairbrush out of her bag. "Or she'll appear to be high on something, but it's all because Esmeralda's birds have woven Lynn Mae's hair into their nest, making her vulnerable to their master's influence."

I can hear Mama talking about Pam now, saying she was never really crazy like people assumed her to be. It was the drugs that forced Pam into a nightmare that she couldn't escape from, also Esmeralda's doing come to find out.

"Mama said something about voodoo dolls in our vision a moment ago," I say, curious about the miniature Raggedy Anne looking toy Dr. Whitmore placed on the table with Mama.

"Yes, I know," Dr. Whitmore says, taking out a silver tray lined with needles of various shapes and sizes.

Netta brushes Mama's hair, removes several strands with the roots still attached and hands them to Dr. Whitmore.

"I didn't think you got down like this, Dr. Whitmore," I say, surprised at his skills. I knew he was the man to see about herbs and other concoctions, but I never took him for a full-fledged working priest in the religion.

"Why? Because I'm an old man?" Dr. Whitmore says with a little sarcasm of his own.

"I didn't say that," I say, watching as he takes a sewing needle and weaves Mama's hair into the doll resting at the crown of her head.

"It's okay, Jayd. I'm used to it. Sexism goes both ways in this line of work." Dr. Whitmore looks at his book and turns the page, explicitly following the directions. "The Religion gives more power to women and rightfully so. But we're equal souls in this work, Jayd."

"Men are the ones good with hunting, be it with voodoo dolls or other methods of trapping folks. It takes the Mothers to cast the nets and reel it all in," Netta says, brushing Mama's hair back into a bun at the nape of her neck. "Right now your grandmother needs to rest. We'll take care of Esmeralda for her."

67

"How did Esmeralda even get to Mama like this?" I ask, baffled that Mama's fallen at the hand of her enemy. Like a naïve child, I always believed that my grandmother was untouchable. Seeing her lying here looking completely defeated shows me just how wrong I've been. I should've kicked Esmeralda's ass a long time ago.

"I taught Esmeralda how to dress voodoo dolls decades ago in Nawlins," Dr. Whitmore says, a southern drawl escaping his usually proper tongue. He looks like he now regrets that tutelage. "Esmeralda forgets that I hold the same power that she does when it comes to the art of making crows sing."

"Can we make a doll for Esmeralda?"

Netta looks at me and beams with pride. "Now you're thinking like a queen, iyawo."

"We will work on that later," Dr. Whitmore says, carefully choosing his next instrument. "When I make my dolls I like to use sewing needles in addition to acupuncture needles for two reasons: Number one, because they come in various lengths, widths and shapes, allowing me to weave in every single thought I want at the exact angle and position that I want it in. Number two, because the art of sewing up a doll is very similar to the art of stitching skin back together. Both require needle, thread, and blood."

Netta takes a small needle from the tray and pricks my grandmother's left middle finger. A small, round drop of blood forms on her fingertip. Netta brings the doll to Mama's skin and wipes it clean on the doll's head. I'm still in awe that we're making a voodoo doll for Mama.

"She's all dressed and ready to go," Netta says, admiring their handiwork.

68

"You will have your grandmother's doll, Jayd so that you can easily access her dreams once you get the hang of it," Dr. Whitmore says, directing Netta to hand it to me. "Whatever you do, don't let her out of your sight."

"How will I get the hang of jumping into my grandmother's thoughts when I can't even keep her and my mom out of my head?" I ask, eyeing the strange doll. I managed to keep my mom from jumping in my head a few times but that was only temporary.

"Ask your ancestors, Jayd," Netta says, touching the five jade bracelets on my wrist, reminding me of our lineage. "You've got everything you need to beat Esmeralda at her own game, once and for all."

"Your grandmother can also help you, Jayd. She's awake on the other side, and more powerful than you can imagine," Dr. Whitmore says, brushing a loose strand from Mama's cheek. "Get her to realize that it's just a dream induced by Esmeralda. It will appear as if she's returned to her young days as the Voodoo Queen of New Orleans. From what I can tell that's where Esmeralda took her with the doll she dressed."

"I guess that's why she was so powerful, and they fought like they were on Game of Thrones," I say, again seeing Mama and Esmeralda battle in the ring. "She and Esmeralda were going hard with their swords." It reminds me of the dream I had of Mama losing her head in the mirror: All of it is beginning to make sense.

"And Esmeralda wants it to stay like that so she can beat Lynn Mae and change the events of the past, making herself the Queen," Dr. Whitmore says, manipulating the needles in Mama's feet. "You can imagine the danger in that, I know."

69

"Dr. Whitmore, are you saying that Esmeralda can change the past with a little doll?" I look at the toy in my hand and realize that it's nothing to play with.

"I'm saying that she can change the present with a small yet very powerful charm, which is even more dangerous. Your grandmother's actions in the past are what can change it, especially if she's in a dream state."

"Dr. Whitmore made a doll to reach Mama's spirit while Esmeralda made one to control her physically," Netta says, making a list of all of the things Mama will need from the house since she's going to be posted up here indefinitely. "We need the other doll to balance Lynn Mae's whole being and bring her back."

"I'll get the other doll, don't worry," I say, holding on tightly to the one in my hand. Esmeralda will never claim victory over any woman in my lineage, not as long as I'm breathing.

"I have every confidence that you will, young queen," Dr. Whitmore says. "Just remember that Esmeralda's the master, and Rousseau tracks down the people she wants to control. Whatever you do don't let Rousseau get to you. Otherwise, you'll be the next voodoo doll she makes."

~ 6 ~
VOODOO DOLLS

Like a good godchild, Mr. Adewale kept watch outside without disturbing our work inside. I didn't know that Mr. Adewale was a full-fledged student of Dr. Whitmore, acupuncture needles and all. How many secrets can one man have?

"You're a witch doctor, too?" I ask, impressed with Mr. Adewale's knowledge. "Just when I think I've got you all figured out you come up with something new to shock me."

"Don't sound so surprised," he says, tying Mama's hair with hemp yarn and then positioning it onto the dolls head. "I was properly trained in the art of all things voodoo, just like you're being trained now."

"Ogunlabi is a very talented priest," Dr. Whitmore says, washing Mama's forehead with lavender oil and another fragrance I don't recognize, but it smells divine. "He will make a wise elder one day."

"How's Lynn Mae doing?" Netta asks, reentering the space with fresh towels. Whatever they did has Mama sleeping like a baby.

"She's just fine, resting peacefully for now," Dr. Whitmore says.

For now? What's that supposed to mean, and exactly how long is my grandmother going to be out of commission?

"How are we going to explain Mama's disappearance to everyone, including our clients in an hour?" I blurt out. Suddenly I'm afraid of life without Mama around on a daily basis. It's as if she's slowly dying right before my eyes and there's nothing that I can do about it. "Not to mention our family?"

71

Dr. Whitmore reaches across Mama's bed and takes my hand. "Do you trust me, Jayd?"

"Yes, I do," I say, near tears. "And more importantly, my grandmother does."

He looks into my eyes and I can remember him stitching up my knee after I cut it wide open running from a dog. I was eight years old, and it seemed like the needle he used to numb my wound was ten feet long. Whatever was inside calmed me down so well that I fell asleep in my grandmother's lap while he patched me. Mama used to call him the fix it man, but Daddy didn't like that too much so she stopped. But I'll always remember Dr. Whitmore as the man who could fix anything, including my grandmother's current state of mind.

"We'll say she went on an emergency trip to New Orleans, which ain't far from the truth," Netta says, wiping the tears from her cheeks. "And we don't know when she'll return."

"Can't she stay awake long enough to at least say good bye to her husband?" I know my mom's already hip to the plan via my thoughts, but Daddy and the boys have no idea of what's going on.

"No one outside of this room can know, for their own sake and for Lynn Mae's," Dr, Whitmore says, letting me go. "Esmeralda has living zombies everywhere and the worst part is that they don't even know it; in the church, at the grocery store, even at your school. Esmeralda's touch is wide-spread and we have to be extremely careful who we talk to."

My grandfather understands Mama's work but I'm not sure how he'd feel about this. When Mama had to go to the hospital last week for her head injury Daddy had a fit and then some, but Mama told me not to tell him where the bird came from. I know he has his suspicions, as does

72

Bryan and Jay, but they know not ask too many questions when it comes to Mama.

"It's dangerous for her to be awake for too long," Netta says, wrapping her right arm around my shoulders. "Rousseau cannot track her scent when she's asleep. He can hear from miles away and catch a scent from her body odor or even the slightest movement she makes. He's a beast and hunts like one, too."

"I see." I miss my grandmother already. I'd give anything for her to be able to invade my mind now: I never thought I'd miss the constant mental intrusions.

"She'll be okay, Jayd," Mr. Adewale says, putting his hand on my left shoulder. "You're grandmother is as tough as they come."

"So was my great-grandmother and all of our mother's before her," I say, looking at my bracelets. "And they were all killed." The tears I've been holding back begin to flow freely as the gravity of this moment sinks in.

"Yes, but not this time," Netta says wiping the tears from my eyes. "Your ancestors never had a fully initiated daughter or granddaughter to help them fight their enemies. You, young lady, are not an infant. You will save your grandmother, and that's all there is to it." Netta picks up her purse, kisses my grandmother on the forehead and heads for the front door. "We need to pick up some things for Lynn Mae before opening the shop. And my son was supposed to drop your car off at the house on his way to work this morning. We'll check back in at the end of the day."

The sun is shining bright this morning, giving us all an idea of just how beautiful a day it's going to be. It's just another Saturday for most, but not for us. My grandmother's sanity is on the line and it's up to me to make sure she doesn't lose it forever.

Netta packed a full overnight bag for Mama explaining to our family that Mama's trip was unexpected and couldn't be avoided. No one asked any questions, not even my grandfather, although I could tell he had a thousand of them. Netta explained to me the importance of keeping Mama clean every day. If she isn't bathed and her clothes changed daily then Rousseau could catch her scent and come for her.

After we closed the shop Netta went back to Mama's bedside while I came back to my grandparents' house to work in the spirit room for the rest of the night so that I could figure this whole thing out. Keenan was upset that I cancelled our plans, but he has to learn patience when it comes to my spirit life, just like my grandfather does with Mama.

All this time I've had it backwards: I learned from Maman Marie's stories that instead of me trying to figure out how to keep Mama and my mom out of my head I should've been learning how to get inside of theirs. Purposefully falling into a dream pattern with my grandmother's not going to be easy but it can be done. I can't stay in her head for too long or else I risk getting caught up in her witch-created reality, too.

"I think I've got it, girl," I say to an alert Lexi who's been my constant companion. Usually she'd be knocked out across the threshold, but without Mama here she's all out of sorts.

Lexi turns her head toward the door and begins to growl.

"What is it, girl?" I ask, looking out of the small window at the top of the door.

74

Lexi's growl grows from low and guttural to a loud and vicious bark. She only reacts this violently toward one individual: Rousseau.

I open the door to find him standing right in front of me as if he rang the bell and was awaiting my answer.

"Bonsoir, mademoiselle," Rousseau says, breathing heavily. "Might I add that you smell absolutely ravishing this evening?" Rousseau looks like he's dressed for a costume party in a formal Colonial suit and top hat. I guess he's also caught back in time with Esmeralda and Mama.

"You don't scare me," I say, confronting Rousseau; the exact opposite of what Dr. Whitmore advised.

"Then you are a fool." Rousseau sniffs the air between us. "I've had mercy on you thus far, little princess. My generosity ends now."

"Touché," I say, taking a step back. His breath smells like the dog he truly is.

"Jayd, mi petite. Such a beautiful young woman," Rousseau says, his shape shifting into a young and still impeccably dressed Creole white man. In this form, he actually resembles Maman's lover, Jeremy's great-grandfather. "In another time I might have considered making you one of my many, many concubines."

"And I might have considered killing you in your sleep," I say, keeping Lexi from charging.

Rousseau belts out an evil laugh. "Such a charming young woman, indeed," he says, touching the edge of his trimmed mustache. In this body he's actually attractive. This must be who Esmeralda sees when she looks at her beast. "I'm just checking on your grandmother. Such an unfortunate incident last weekend, oui?"

75

"Oui, very unfortunate. But, as you know, my grandmother's a strong woman. Thank you for your concern." I attempt to close the door but our unwelcomed guest persists on.

"Are you sure, mi petite? I sensed that she was in dire straits when I prayed over our enemies this morning," he says, attempting to look over the threshold, but the Legba shrine by the door stops him cold. No one is allowed in the spirit room without an invitation from Mama or myself. Even Rousseau respects Legba's power to protect and serve impartial justice when needed.

"I find it very interesting that you pray over your prey."

By the scowl on his face I'd say Rousseau isn't impressed by my wit. He repeatedly sniffs the air between us much like Lexi does when she's looking for buried treats. "I don't take too kindly to liars, Jayd." Rousseau calls me by name instead of the various pet names he's conjured up for me: I must've hit a nerve.

"Here I am thinking that you can't be lied to," I say, sniffing at Rousseau in return. "I was sure that was impossible with your astute hound dog skills and all."

"Careful young queen," Rousseau says, stretching his palms open and displaying his yellow claws. "Heavy is the head that wears the crown. And since the reigning queen seems to be M.I.A. that makes your head the new target."

"Is that a threat?" I ask. Lexi's by my side, ready to leap at my command.

"Oui, mademoiselle. It most certainly is," Rousseau says, momentarily mirroring my great-grandfather, Jean Paul, also his godfather. "And I wouldn't take it lightly if I were you. My queen does not make empty threats."

"You can tell your witch of a queen to kiss my ass."

"Indeed, I will relay the message and quite possibly grant your wish if you like," Rousseau says, displaying his fangs as if to attract me like a peacock spreading his tail. What the hell?

I look down at Lexi who's about to snap. "You're way out of line. Get the hell out of our yard before I let her loose on you!" I scream loudly, hoping somebody's inside the main house, but on a Saturday night that's highly unlikely.

"Go ahead," Rousseau says, manifesting a toothpick to pick his overgrown teeth. "It's a bit early for my midnight snack but I can make an exception for you, j'adore."

"Rousseau," Esmeralda calls out of her back door. "Mon amor?" she says, wondering where her love is. Interesting that she can't seem to track her man-pet eventhough he's right next-door.

"Until next time, mon petit," he says, vanishing as swiftly as he appeared. Why is Rousseau over here bothering me without Esmeralda's knowledge? Something else is going on with him; I can feel it in my bones.

"Guess I'm not done after all," I say, rubbing Lexi's neck.

She's still vexed but calming down.

"I guess it's just you, me and the ancestors tonight, girl."

"One day I'm not going to be here and you're going to wish that you were a better student."
-Mama
Drama High, volume one: The Fight

~ 7 ~
HAVE MERCY

Last night I slept in the spirit room not only because I was too exhausted to drive home, but also because I feel safer in here than anywhere else. Rousseau is straight tripping and is taking me right along with him. I did a little more digging on his powers and what he was like as a young man in several of his incarnations. He always comes back to New Orleans, always with Esmeralda's lineage, and always desiring to join the Williams' bloodline by any means necessary.

Instead of thinking like me, which is to just haul off and kick his ass for coming at me last night, I decided to ask WWMD: What Would Mama Do? I decided that in this case she'd enlist some outside unconventional help. I'll have to make a trip to Long Beach to visit the old witch doctor Mama calls on when she needs something handled gutter style. The ugly has to get done even if we're not the ones to do it. Mama says the religion, like life, is built on two main staples: blood and shit. We deal with the blood; the old witch doctor deals with the shit. He'll help me get back at Esmeralda and Rousseau through their weakest links, Misty and Emilio, without Dr. Whitmore's, Netta's or Mama's knowledge.

My cell vibrates with yet another text from Rah. It's his third message today and it's only nine in the morning. "What up, Jayd. I know you got the letter from my attorney with the court date. Call me back, please."

Dude is on my jock something fierce. Yesterday's walking dream

78

quest with Mama was a clear indication that I need to focus on my own shit right now, not my friends and their self-manifested drama. I'll text him back later if I'm feeling charitable.

"Jayd, a word," Rah says, scaring the hell out of me as I walk toward my car from the back yard.

"Rah, what the hell are you doing creeping up on me?" I ask, noticing his immaculate Acura parked across the street. The '93 coupe will never go out of style.

"I'm sorry I scared you but we need to talk," Rah says, walking behind me. I have to be in Long Beach in thirty minutes and don't have time for one of our regular arguments.

"It's not a good time," I say, unlocking the car door. I place my purse and overnight bag in the backseat ready to roll. "And how did you know I'd be here?"

"I ran into Bryan last night playing ball."

I forget that dudes talk just as much as chicks do.

"Jayd, look. I know I screwed up again but you have to forgive me, please." Rah sounds so sincere, but doesn't he always? And I continuously have mercy on his lying ass, but not this time.

"Rah, as often as you make penance I could mistake you for being Catholic," I say, slamming the back door shut. After finding out about him and Trish faking a happy home for the judge, I'm really not moved by his words.

"Funny, Jayd. Real funny," Rah says, unamused. "At least you haven't lost your sense of humor."

"No I haven't, but I did loose one of my oldest and best friends over some nonsense," I say, attempting to get in my mom's car but this dude refuses to budge.

79

"You haven't lost me as a friend, Jayd," he says, touching my left cheek with the back of his hand. His touch still sends a chill down my spine. "Do you think I would've put you down on my character witness list if you did? I need you now more than ever."

I back away from his advance. "Rah, we've already been through this before," I say, remembering the last time I helped him gain temporary custody of Rahima. This time is for keeps. "One advantage that I have over every other female in your life is that I've known you the longest. I know you too well and have been down this very same road with you before."

"What the hell are talking about? We've never been here before—ever," Rah says, completely vexed. "I'm trying to do the right thing by my child and you're making this shit all about us when it's not. It's about me trying to be a good father to my little girl by keeping her crazy ass mama away from her."

"You always find a way to make yourself the victim," I say, returning the heat. "You always find a way to make everything all about you when it's not. Damn it, Rah. Don't you see how you're just as big of an ass as Sandy is when it comes to getting your way?"

"That's low, Jayd." Rah's pain is written all over his face. "I don't know if I can forgive that shit."

"I'm not asking you to," I say, feeling even more determined to get away from him. "I don't need your mercy, Rah. Never have."

Rah stares at me as if he doesn't recognize me, the same girl he's known and loved since junior high school. I love him, too, but enough's enough.

"Good morning, Rah, Jayd," Daddy, says, parking his Cadillac in one of our two driveways. He exits the vehicle and kisses me on the

80

cheek. Daddy usually comes home between sermons when he can to catch his breath. Dealing with an entire congregation of needy folks and over-loyal women can work even the holiest of man's nerves.

"Pastor James," Rah says, extending his hand. "It's nice to see you again, sir."

"Always good to see you, too, son. How's that beautiful little girl of yours?"

"Growing every day, sir," Rah says, a large smile spreading across his ebony face, replacing the anger that was there a moment ago. Anyone can see how much he loves Rahima by the way his whole being lights up at the mere mention of her name.

"I'm glad I caught you, Jayd," Daddy says. "I want you to come by the church this afternoon. We're holding the first of a monthly program for recently paroled teens after the last service."

"Daddy, I wish I could come but I've got errands to run for Mama." Why do all of the men in my life always need me when it's convenient for them?

"But your grandmother's in New Orleans, Jayd. What errands could you possibly have to run for her that can't wait?" Daddy looks at me quizzically, almost tricking me into a confession. I know he knows something else is up.

"Okay, I'll be there." I glance at Esmeralda's house and feel someone's eyes on me. The next time either Esmeralda or Rousseau rear their ugly heads I'm going to have something for their asses.

"That's my Tweet," Daddy says, winking at me. He must very proud to call me by his pet name for me. "See you this afternoon. Good to see you as always, Rah," Daddy says, jogging up the front porch steps.

"Yes sir," Rah says. He returns his attention to me, still shocked by my lack of empathy.

"Here, Rah," I say, removing the gold necklace and ankh charm from around my neck—it was one of the best birthday presents I've ever received but I can't keep it or anything else he's gifted me with. "I'll give you the cell back as soon as I get a replacement."

"You better not even try to give back anything I ever gave you, girl. Everything I did for you was out of love. Still is." He attempts to replace the necklace but I move away, and finally manage to get in the car.

"I'm done constantly jumping through hoola hoops to be in your life, Rah. You're on your own this time." I start the engine, grateful to have my ride back.

"Damn Jayd, it's like that?" Rah asks, raising his voice. I haven't seen him this upset with me in a long time. "So I guess I'll just tell Rahima and Kamal that you're not in our lives, again."

"You can't manipulate me into feeling guilty about something that's all your doing, Rah. But it's nice to know that you haven't changed a bit. Now I know I'm doing the right thing." I close the car door and lock it.

"Jayd, girl, get out of the car. We're not done," Rah says, knocking on the driver's side window. He should know better than to try and bully me.

I wave good-bye to Rah but doubt that he can see me through the tinted windows. I'm sure he gets the message now that I've pulled away from the curb. I know I'm supposed to be all forgiving and turn the other cheek, but I've run out of patience with Rah. Maybe the old witch doctor's got something to help me forget about his ass, too.

My trip to Long Beach was cut short because of my morning drama. The priest wasn't happy with my tardiness and let me know it as soon as I approached his house. He gave me a bag full of herbs and oils with instructions to follow and kept it moving. It's not easy trying to do all of this without my grandmother here to guide me every step of the way. I'm used to doing little things to help my friends and myself out, but never work on Mama. I hope I get it right the first time because once Esmeralda and Rousseau get wind of my bag of tricks I doubt that I'll have a second chance.

"Jayd, so nice of you to come," Rita, one of the church elders says as I enter the dining hall. There are only two girls and ten boys present at the meeting including G, Mickey's man.

I haven't spoken to Mickey since she informed me of her intention to act as his alibi for the night of Pam's murder. I agree he was wrongly accused of the crime and know for a fact that he didn't do it, but she's wrong to lie for him no matter what her reasoning might be. And Mickey's even more wrong to get back with G and leave Nigel out of the parenting equation. I have a feeling Mickey's not going to be able to get away with her moves this time around. If it's one thing I know about Nigel it's that he doesn't give up.

"That's what I'm talking about," G says as I step inside. Had I known I was coming to the church before I got dressed this morning I would've opted not to wear my hip hugging jeans and tank top. It's apparent that these dudes can't handle it. "There is a God after all." G winks at me as I take a seat next to my grandfather's chair at the head of the table. I guess he was released after Mickey's false confession and placed on parole for one of his many other legal violations.

83

"Hell yeah there is," another guy says, licking his lips my way and showing off his grill. Yuck.

I wish dudes would get it through their egotistical skulls that females don't like that shit. There's nothing sexy to me at all about a boy who let's his drawers hang out of his low-riding pants, or one who blings out his mouth instead of going to the dentist to get his teeth cleaned.

Daddy's still inside the sanctuary talking to a couple who's planning to have their wedding here in a few months. I wish he'd hurry up so I can get on with my day. This is not how I wanted to spend my Sunday afternoon. I have three clients lined up for this evening, not to mention that I've been neglecting my budding relationship with Keenan.

The church ladies are busy preparing juice and cookies like it's summer bible camp instead of a meeting for recent parolees, but I can't blame them. Once a mother always a mother, I suppose. Even Mama has sympathy for G. She and Netta secured his attorney and were willing to go all the way to the Supreme Court to prove that he didn't murder Pam if necessary.

"Why y'all looking at her like she's laying across the table getting served?" one of the two rough looking broads present says, staring me down. "She ain't even all that, probably still a virgin."

"Even better," G says, smiling. "I haven't had fresh meat in a long time."

That's the last thing I need him to visualize happening. I want to smack the chick for putting that thought out there, but she looks like she'd have no problem beating my ass down in front of God and everybody else. The energy is already thick in here, like they could knock daddy out and run a train on all of the women if they really wanted to. But luckily there's an officer posted by the back door to make sure everything stays chill.

"Okay, young men. Listen up," Daddy says, slamming his Holy Bible down on the table, catching everyone's attention.

Rita joins us at the table with a bible of her own.

"Damn, Reverend Massa. Ain't no need for all that shit," G says, making the other dudes around the table laugh. He lacks the natural good sense filter most of us were born with.

I know he didn't just call my grandfather Massa like he's living in the big house and they're on the plantation. I'm glad they're getting a kick out of this because pastor or not, Daddy doesn't take any mess. I can tell by the heat rising out of my grandfather's collar that he's about to bring down the wrath of God on these unsuspecting so-called gangsters. Rita and I look at each other, take a deep breath and shake our heads: The shit's about to go down and we both know it.

"Young man, I've had just about all the disrespect I can take from you. We're here for you and this is how you act, like a little kid?" Daddy says, gesturing at Rita and me. "If it weren't for Rita and your parole officer we wouldn't be here. Consider yourselves blessed."

The parolees shift in their seats as their parole officer makes his way over to our table.

"Is everything all right, Pastor James?" he says, his right fist balled up tightly ready to beat the respect back into any one of these fools if need be. I wish he would just take a pole upside G's head. That would solve so many problems in my book. It was nice when he was locked up. All G's good for is terrorizing our neighborhood. How Mickey ever hooked up with him is beyond me.

"Yes, Jamal. Everything is fine. We're just getting some things straight. Isn't that right, Gary?"

Gary? Who the hell is Gary?

"Yeah, we cool," Mickey's man says, shocking the hell out of me and then some.

All the years I've known G I've never known anyone to call him by his name. Hell, I thought maybe he didn't know it even if he had been given one. He walks around the neighborhood calling himself G for gangster, like his mama took one look at him when he was born and knew that's all he would ever be. But now we know the G actually stands for Gary. Wow. I can't wait to tell everyone about this discovery.

"Now, like I was saying. Ms. Rita thinks it's a good idea that we talk once a month to get your spirits back on track and I couldn't agree more. I take it personally that so many of the young women and men baptized in my church have now been baptized by the judicial system. I'm here to see that no matter what happens you become the grown women and men you keep claiming to be. My granddaughter, Jayd is here to help as well."

I don't know what it is he expects me to do but I'm here, even if I don't want to be. Daddy's always trying to get me more involved in his church as if I don't have enough responsibilities to deal with.

"Ain't nobody claiming nothing," G says, squirming in his seat. "I am a grown ass man. Ask your girl," he says to me, grinning.

"Have you no shame, young man?" Rita says, getting up out of her seat and smacking G on the leg with her church fan. "Watch your mouth around Pastor James. He's a man of the cloth. Act like you've got the good sense God gave you and use it to shut up."

I can't help but snicker at little Ms. Rita checking the big and almighty G. She's a little old lady with a lot of spunk and one of the few church ladies that doesn't work all of Mama's nerves.

"Being a grown man is about more than getting this so-called respect you all claim is owed to you. It's about owning up to the responsibilities that life brings your way. It's about honoring yourself and those around you. It's about honoring your word."

G catches my eye and makes an inappropriate tongue gesture. Before I can check his nasty ass my site locks onto his and I'm in his mind. I can see him walking past Esmeralda's house late at night, her crow landing on his shoulder and pecking him in the neck. G swings at the bird but it flies away before he can get to it. Once the bird is safely inside, Esmeralda takes the blood from its beak, drops it into a vile and then mixes it with something else. She then places the liquid onto a male voodoo doll and pins a tiny satchel onto its body. There are also four other dolls next to his who remind me of Misty, her mother, Emilio and his godfather, Hector, a priest in the religion who also has a bone to pick with Mama.

The image skips to G selling ecstasy and other pills on the street. After he collects the money, Esmeralda manipulates him through the doll to bring the money back to her house. She gives him a bottle of pills and sends him on his way with G none the wiser that she's actually pimping his ass out. When he finds out what's really going on all hell's going to break loose.

"Jayd, did you hear me?" Daddy asks, snapping me back into the present moment. "I want you to lead the reading. We're in First Corinthians."

I look at G who doesn't seem to notice that I just left his head. Do I tell him what I just saw? I don't know what to do with the information but it must've been given to me for a reason. I'll have to wait and ask Mama when she wakes up this evening. As always, she'll know what to do.

"Nature's in all things. We can't be separate from creation because we are a part of it, including our minds."
-Jayd
Drama High, volume 10: Culture Clash

~ 8 ~
A BLESSING AND A CURSE

After the church session is over I rush around the corner to Dr. Whitmore's office. I know that he and Netta are in the back working feverishly on a way to help Mama. I have to tell them about my vision right now before any of it fades. I know it sounds far-fetched and I can't prove a thing yet but they need to know exactly what we're dealing with. Mama's sleep walking vision was on point. Esmeralda's taken her war with Mama from the spirit world to the streets, damn the innocent victims.

"It's happening again, Jayd!" Netta screams at me upon entering the otherwise serene space. "Esmeralda's got her sleepwalking, that evil witch!"

"How?" I ask, scared as all get out. I take out Mama's voodoo doll and empty the contents of the bag the old priest made for me to throw off Rousseau's skills. Mama's going buck wild and speaking in tongues like she's under the influence of the Holy Spirit; we know there's nothing holy about this power.

Dr. Whitmore recognizes the root worker's instruments and cuts his eyes at me. I know there's history there but now is not the time to dig. "You're the only one who has a chance at reaching your grandmother in this state."

"But how?" Last time Mama snatched me into her vision and that shit hurt. I don't want to do that again.

"Jayd, relax," Dr. Whitmore says, his voice even and steady.

"Focus all of your energy on calming her breath. Willfully fall to sleep and dream walk with your grandmother. Her life depends on it." Dr. Whitmore lights a few incense sticks and dims the lights. How does he always remain so calm?

"Here, baby," Netta says, ushering me toward the massage table. "Lay down and do what the doctor says. I've got Lynn Mae." Netta follows my grandmother around to make sure that she doesn't hurt herself. In this state Mama's liable to run through a glass window or better yet attack one of us. Damn Esmeralda for this shit.

"Okay," I say, doing as I'm told. "I need to spread these herbs around the room. It'll help us both."

Netta looks at Dr. Whitmore who reluctantly nods his head in affirmation. She takes the contents and sprinkles them around the room.

"Listen," Dr. Whitmore says, softly ringing the brass bell. "When it rings, breathe in. When it's quiet, breathe out and fall into a deep sleep."

"Just like that?" I say, closing my eyes. Falling instantaneously into a deep sleep isn't that easy at night let alone during the day.

"Yes, Jayd. Just like that." Dr. Whitmore says, standing at my feet.

The first couple of times the bell rings I can't relax. My heart is pulsating and I'm breaking out into a cold sweat. I'm scared of falling into the dream. I'm also afraid of failing Mama. The third time's the charm: I'm inside of Mama's dream world and it doesn't look so bad. It's actually quite peaceful, contrary to what it appears to be in reality.

"It's about time you showed up," Mama says. She looks young and vibrant, the complete opposite of Esmeralda's youthful transformation, which is more reminiscent of a harlot's revolution. "I've missed my grandbaby."

90

"I've missed you, too," I say, wrapping my arms around Mama. It's then that I realize we're standing on top of the same alligator she was riding in her last vision. Oh hell no.

"Don't be afraid, Jayd. He won't bite."

The hell he won't. I look at the large reptile and plan my escape without us becoming his dinner. "Mama, I need you to come with me," I say, grabbing Mama's hand tightly like I used to do when I was a little girl crossing the street. "This isn't your dream; it's Esmeralda's."

"Oh chile, please," Mama says, tossing her head back and allowing her wildly curly hair to flow freely across her shoulders. Mama's always stunning but I've never seen her glow like this before. "You don't think that I know the difference between a dream and a nightmare? Look at me; I'm gorgeous! Esmeralda would never make me dream like this."

She has a good point but she's still wrong. "Look, I don't know why she's allowing you to appear in your prime but I'm telling you, Mama. This isn't your dream. Rousseau hunted you down and Esmeralda took over. Trust me, we need to go. Now!"

"What did I tell you about minding your business, little girl?" Esmeralda says, rising out of the water. She's walking on top of the water, heading straight for us.

"Oh my," Mama says, staring at her nemesis shell-shocked. "But I look so beautiful," Mama catches her reflection in the river and begins to comb her fingers through her hair ignoring the danger we're in. What the hell is wrong with her?

"Mama, watch out!" The alligator rises out of the water at Esmeralda's command. I realize that we're actually riding Rousseau.

I toss Mama off of his back and safely onto the shore.

"Not so fast, my pretty," he says, charging out of the water toward

91

me.

"Rousseau, don't let them get away!" Esmeralda shouts from the center of the river. "I need them in the water!"

"Mama, wake up!" I yell, hoping she snaps out of it before it's too late, but it's no use. She's too busy staring at herself in the reflection, reminding me of Maman's warning: We never know what lies beneath the water.

"Oh shit!" I say, losing my grip. Instead of falling into the water like I did in my own narcissistic vision, I catch myself and jump right back on.

Rousseau changes from an alligator into a huge crocodile and attempts to toss me into the water. He keeps changing forms, trying to throw me off of his back but I'm not going anywhere. He could morph into a goddamn dinosaur for all I care. I'll keep riding him like the mule that he is until my grandmother wakes up.

"Mama, please! Stop looking at yourself and wake up. Please!"

Mama looks at me and stares. "Do you think I should dye my hair? There's so much gray."

Oh hell. She's really gone now. Then I remember the words the old witch doctor told me to repeat:

"The only reality is the one we make. In this dream world it's give and take." I say the words quietly at first. With each repetition they become louder and more forceful.

"Shut her up, Rousseau!" Esmeralda screams, flying toward my grandmother who's still caught up in her own reflection. I've never seen her like this before.

I repeat the mantra again, this time directing the words directly at Esmeralda. She should know better than to underestimate my determination. I hop off of Rousseau's back, push Esmeralda out of my *way, and force Mama's forehead to mine like she did to me; our powers are united. My eyes begin to glow with Mama's sight. I look straight into Esmeralda's crystal blue eyes and shoot her look right back at her. This isn't the first time I've given her a taste of her own poison.*

Rousseau, concerned with his master's health, halts his attack on us and morphs back into the man beast that he is. "Mon amour," he says, holding her in his arms. She's aging rapidly, changing back into her true self.

"My head!" Esmeralda screams, covering her ears. The headaches her eyes bring on are no joke. I haven't had one in a while and don't care to share hers. "Make her stop!"

I pull my grandmother away and force her to look into my eyes. "Mama, you must wake up."

Instead of looking at me Mama looks straight through me, catching her reflection in my eyes. "What a lovely vision you are, my sweet," she says. I don't know if she's talking about her or me but it really doesn't matter. I lock onto my own reflection in her emerald eyes and force her back into reality.

"Jayd, are you okay?" Netta says, holding me by the shoulders. "Lynn Mae is awake."

"I'm okay, I think," I say, shaking off the bad experience. I sit up on the table and stare at my grandmother across the room. She looks like a frightened child. "Mama, are you okay?"

Mama stares at me but doesn't answer. She looks around the Chinese medicine shop completely confused.

"Lynn Mae, drink this," Dr. Whitmore says, passing her a small jade cup filled with green tea and a little something extra.

Mama dutifully takes the cup without saying a word.

93

"Lynn Mae, it's okay," Netta says, walking Mama over toward the futon against the wall. They both sit down in silence.

"Jayd, you should have some as well." Dr. Whitmore passes me the drink and I gulp it down.

"It's vanity," Mama finally says, barely audible. "She's using Oshune's vanity against me and her other victims."

"You think?" I say, still aggravated that Mama took me for the ride of my life. If I never see another river again it'll be too soon.

"I'm sorry, honey. I wasn't aware of my actions. I feel like I had a mental breakdown," Mama says, rubbing her temples. She attempts to get up but Dr. Whitmore forces her to stay seated.

"Ain't nothing wrong with a little breakdown every now and then. It's good for the soul. After the breakdown comes clarity. Always. Every time." Netta pats Mama's hands, noting that her cuticles need tending to. "Don't you worry about a thing, Lynn Mae. My sisters will be here tomorrow to help with the shop. And I won't let them try to run a damned thing like they did when we left on our last adventure. They know it's us and nobody else. And Jayd will be there to keep them in line, too."

Netta fights back her tears and I know how she feels. Mama's not looking good and we all know she can't tolerate another dream snatching like that.

"I had a vision through G's eyes earlier," I say, remembering the cold sensation. "G is another one under her influence. Esmeralda's selling drugs and using his body to do it. I have a feeling she's also setting him up for Pam's murder to save herself."

94

"Jayd, are you sure?" Dr. Whitmore asks. He further checks out the contents of the brown paper bag the old priest gave me, planning his next move.

"Yes, positive." I look at him and shake my head in affirmation. "Misty, her mother, Emilio and his godfather are also her mules. She's got dolls for each of them."

"Jayd, are you positive?" Netta asks, but she knows I'm telling the truth. My dreams never lie even when I wish they would. "If this is what she's been up to we've got to stop her now before someone else gets hurt."

"I can't be sure, but I think she's selling ecstasy and other party drugs. She's using G's street connects to get her product out. Misty and Emilio bring new clients to her. I don't know Hector's place in all of this yet, but she's been very busy from what my vision said." I've heard of every block having a candy lady who sells sweets out of her home, but this is an entirely different spin on the neighborhood staple.

"Rousseau's her watchdog and enforcer, no doubt," Mama says, staring off into the distance. "Esmeralda's days are numbered."

"Lynn Mae, what are we going to do? Your children and mine are in danger if that heffa gets away with murder."

Netta's right about that. If my uncles find out Esmeralda's got the hot shit in her house they're liable to either become clients, sales representatives, or try to rob her, all of which will be the end of their lives in one way or another.

"Esmeralda," Dr. Whitmore says into his hand full of cowrie shells. He also does readings? There's so much about the good doctor that I don't know. "Jayd, have any of your friends experienced any unusual challenges lately?" he asks, reading the shells.

95

"Yes, all of them, but that's nothing new," I say, thinking about my fallen crew. "My friends always have plenty of drama around them."

Nellie's in an abusive relationship and lying about it. Nigel and Mickey are at war with one another, and Rah's battling for custody of his daughter. Chase is cool for the time being, but Jeremy is caught up in Cameron's nightmare. It's just another day in the life of my motley clique and me.

"That drama, as you call it, is indicative of a curse," Dr. Whitmore says, pointing at the mat with the ten shells facing upward. "Ofun Mafun means you have been cursed. Esmeralda knows she can't get to you directly but she can destroy those around you."

"What?" I ask, confused. "Why would she go after my friends when Mama's her true target? My friends can't do anything for her."

"All of your grandmother's friends are in this room," Netta says, ushering around. "Esmeralda can't get to us, so she went for the next best thing. She is going to attack you one friend at a time until it's all said and done."

"I think you should take some time to work on protecting your friends the best way you know how," Dr. Whitmore says, passing me the near-empty bag of goodies. "Esmeralda has no mercy, Jayd. She will ruthlessly dismantle your life brick by brick until you go absolutely insane and take your friends down with you. You won't be able to separate your dreams from reality. The two worlds will collide and it'll feel like you're in a drug-induced haze."

"That's exactly what it felt like inside of my dream," Mama says, sipping the last of her tea. "I was high on narcissism, and it felt damned good."

"Esmeralda's dream, not yours," I say, correcting her.

96

Mama was on a trip like I've never witnessed. It must be how Pam felt when she was high: You couldn't tell her that she didn't look good walking down the street, her raggedy sandals loudly click-clacking against the sidewalk as she approached Mama's house for a plate of food. I could kill Esmeralda for going after my grandmother through Pam, and I will kill her if she doesn't get the message through me.

"What a bitch," Netta says, rising from the futon to help Dr. Whitmore set up for Mama's head cleansing.

"Yes, she is," Mama agrees. "And this is only the beginning." Mama stares at me as if she sees something I'm not yet privy to. Whatever it is has her scared and that frightens me. "Jayd, I'm sorry all of this is falling on your shoulders but I promise, you can handle it. You're much stronger than you think."

I needed to hear that. In this moment a sistah is filled with doubt, fear and dread. I told Rousseau a lie last night when I said I wasn't afraid of him. In all honesty, he scares the shit out of me. And knowing that he and Esmeralda have me and Mama right where they want us is a bit more than I can take no matter how much faith Mama may have in me. I'm angry enough to fight, but without Mama operating at full capacity I may be in over my head.

"A rich ghetto bitch is the worst kind there is, I swear."
- Jayd
Drama High, volume 14: So, So Hood

~ 9 ~
BULLIES AND BITCHES

My clients were not happy with my tardiness yesterday evening, but once I finished hooking up their heads they forgot all about my being late. I spent the remainder of the night looking through the spirit book for ways to keep Esmeralda away from my friends. Because I'm the first one in my lineage born with the gift through my dreams there's no precedent for stopping the bitch with my sight.

I used the rest of the herbs the old priest gave me to keep Rousseau off of Mama's scent while Dr. Whitmore made several Legba stones to surround Mama with. As long as she stays inside of his shop she'll be fine. She can stay awake for a few hours but still has to remain asleep for the majority of the day.

I, of course, can't tell Mickey and Nellie what's really going on but need to find a way to warn them nonetheless. Nigel and Rah have always been supportive of the way I roll but never got too much into exactly what it is that I do. Jeremy's really the only person with an open enough mind to listen to me, but we're not exactly on friendly terms. He knows that I'm dating Keenan and he's caught up with Cameron. That doesn't mean we can't still be friends at some point, just not today.

Knowing Jeremy he probably skipped school to surf this morning. It's a perfect, sunny beach day in Redondo and most of the rich, carefree students are missing in action, including Chase.

"Que paso, chica?" Maggie says, standing in the lunch line behind me. We share a big hug.

"Not much, Maggie. Did you get your dress for Homecoming yet?" I ask, knowing she's excited about the ASU nomination. I can't wait to see her win the crown in two weeks. With all of my drama at home I've been a little out of it at school.

"Mi abuelita is making it. Oh Jayd, it's going to be magnificent, just like my quincinera dress, recuerdo?" Maggie's eyes are glistening she's so caught up in the festivities and I'm glad for it. She deserves to be queen and I'm going to do everything in my power to see that it happens.

"Do I remember," I say, looping my arm through her bent elbow. "How could I forget the biggest party I've ever been to for a girl turning fifteen?" I'm teasing Maggie but really, her party and dress would've put most weddings to shame.

"Jayd, how could you?" Nellie screams from across the courtyard, charging toward us.

"Oh shit," Maggie says, exclaiming my sentiments exactly. "Here comes the bruja of South Bay High."

I giggle at Maggie's description of Nellie, but lately she has been acting like a witch.

"How dare you support some Mexican from around the way when you're supposed to be my best friend?"

Laura and crew are right behind Nellie, each of them in full bitch mode.

"First of all, Mickey's your best friend, not me," I say, even if she did call on me for help the other night. Everyone at home and at school knows that if it weren't for Mickey, Nellie would've been beat down a long time ago. "And second of all, your ignorant, racist ass attitude is exactly why I would never support you running for a damned thing."

99

"Tell her, Jayd," Maggie says, tightening her grip in support.

"No one was talking to you, Maggie," Nellie says. She's not a bad ass at all, but with the white chick crew behind her she thinks she's got some swag.

Mickey's been scarce since Nigel threatened to take her child away from her, so Nellie's been a bit out of control and working my last damned nerve. Let me check this chick right now before Maggie slaps the shit out of her.

"Nellie, when you won the princess spot last year you morphed into a completely different beast, and you were already enough of a heffa to deal with. We're still getting over that shit and now you want to be queen? It's bad enough you're a cheerleader—by default may I remind you—now this. When will you learn?"

I know that was a bit harsh but I'm telling the truth and everybody knows it. Nellie can't handle being the popular girl. The bitch in her has way too much power over the sweet Nellie that's so hard to see.

"I knew you were jealous of me being a cheerleader after you got kicked off of the team! I knew it!" Nellie screams spit she's so worked up. "And now that I'm back where I belong you can't handle it. You're such a fake it's disgusting to watch."

The line continues to move Maggie and me right along with it. I can cuss Nellie out and get my grub on at the same time.

"Nellie, please. You didn't even have my leftovers; Misty did, as usual," I say, reminding her of how she inherited the spot on the team. "You gladly accepted thirds because you want so badly to be something you're not. Don't you see that, Nellie? These same girls are laughing at you behind you're back every chance they get." Laura and her groupies blush at the truth. I know how they operate from my time

100

in ASB, lest they forget. "And speaking of chances, you outdid yourself ruining the one real relationship you ever had, and with one of my actual best friends nonetheless." Chase was too good for her and I'm glad he finally bowed out of that uneven relationship.

"Again, jealous of me because I had something you only wished you could've had," Nellie says, flinging her blonde streaked weave over her right shoulder. "How's it feel to be the only virgin left in the world, Jayd? Next to nuns, of course."

I should slap this trick where she stands but I can't because then she would use that against me, no doubt. Who the hell does she think she is talking to me like this? If I weren't a child of God, Nellie would be picking herself up from off the ground right now, I promise.

"Being a virgin isn't a crime, Nellie. It's better than being a promiscuous hoe." So what if I'm the only person I know who hasn't given up the cookies yet. Is that something to be ashamed of?

"Okay, Dr. Drew," Nellie says, not backing down. What's with her today? Is the friend I picked up in the middle of the night when her punk ass boyfriend left her stranded turning against me a part of the curse Dr. Whitmore warned me about?

"She's cray cray, Jayd," Maggie says, passing me my nacho combo. "Vamonos, mija. It's almost time for fifth period anyway."

"No, not cray. Crazy," I say, following Maggie away from the lunch line. "Use all of the alphabets when talking about Nellie."

"Haters! I'm winning, bitches," Nellie says to our backs.

Maggie gives her a one finger wave good bye and I completely ignore her out-of-control ass. Where is Mickey when this chick needs saving? Maybe Mr. Adewale can calm her ass down in class. Unfortunately I have to see her again in a few minutes.

101

"It looks like the first fight of the year is about to happen," Maggie says, pointing to two freshmen circling each other like Pit bulls in the main lunch quad. This should be interesting.

"I'm just glad it's not me," I say, making Maggie smile. She and her crew have become consistent members at the African Student Union meetings this year, unlike my own crew. They've fallen out of the club one by one, all except for Chase who's always present. I wish Emilio would bounce but that'll never happen, and Mr. Adewale still has hope that his soul can be saved. I hope it happens before I choke Emilio out.

"You ain't gone fight me, fool," the shorter of the two guys says. "Look at you. You was talking all that shit earlier. Now say something, punk." If they do end up fighting it'll be two less for the already miniscule black population at South Bay. The administration will have no problem kicking them to the curb.

"Man, I'm not about to fight you," the taller dude says, but it's too late. All that talk has instigated payment his body has to cash out.

Without hesitation, the short one pops dude in the jaw. Stunned, he grabs his bloodied mouth and runs off in the opposite direction.

"I bet that'll teach you to talk shit, you little bitch."

Shorty looks around the crowded courtyard as if to say, "Who got next?" We all watch him walk away like nothing happened.

High school reminds me of prison in several ways. One way is the need to be the alpha male on the yard. By this shorter fool challenging this taller cat to a fight he's solidified his status for the entire year, perhaps for the rest of his high school career. He'll be known as someone not to mess with. Too bad for his sparring partner there can only be one winner. The loser will be teased all year long. Each school

102

year is already too long if you ask me, and this freshman's just got extra time added onto his.

"It's bad enough the loser had to run away, but did you see his backpack?" Nellie says. "I think it had cartoon characters on it. Is he still in middle school or what?" Only she would notice a fashion mistake in the middle of a dramatic event.

"What are you laughing at?" Laura asks the new girl, Marcia, out of the blue. "You like you just got dropped off by a dump truck coming from the Salvation Army."

Marcia doesn't say a word. She looks as shocked by the comment as the tall dude did by the punch.

"Uh oh. The bitch brigade has a new chew toy. See you later, mami," Maggie says, walking away toward her class.

"Seriously. Did you know you were coming to school this morning?" Laura continues with her clique right behind her, as usual. "You look like you're going to collect bottles from the recycling bin." Laura tosses her empty water bottle at Marcia, giving her girls a good laugh. That was a bit harsh, even for the queen bitch herself.

"What's wrong, Laura? Didn't have your morning ration of bitches brew?" I say, causing a few reluctant bystanders to snicker.

"Yes, as a matter of fact I did. But that still doesn't excuse the fact that this girl, if you can call her that, didn't even try to get dressed this morning. Do you know how lucky you are to be at South Bay High? They probably didn't even have text books at your last school, did they Lassie?"

Nellie laughs and I can't take it anymore. Who the hell does she think she is?

103

Marcia looks shocked at Laura's bitter rant, and that's not even as nasty as the girl can get. Marcia's going to have a hard time if she thinks this is a passing occurrence. Much like the young dude who just lost the fight, Marcia's time at Drama High could be determined by how she handles herself in this very moment. So far it's not looking so good, and I can't stand by and watch her go down without a fight. She doesn't seem like the type of girl who sticks up for herself and that's unfortunate because she'll have to do that on the regular if she plans on surviving around here.

"Laura, go suck on an Ex-lax and sit down somewhere," I say, standing next to Marcia. "And Nellie, just a couple of years ago you were the new girl being bullied by the mean chicks, and now you're one of them. If it weren't for Mickey you'd have a completely different story to tell about your first year at South Bay High."

"That's your problem, Jayd. You're always sticking up for the strays. Who do you think you are: Captain Save-a-Rat?"

If I could, I'd slap Nellie clear across the face for saying some stupid shit like that to me. I have my eyes on the prize of graduating from this tired-ass school in eight months and nothing's going to stop me, but I've always hated bullies and can't tolerate anyone getting bullied in my presence.

"Nellie, sit down with all that stupidity," I say, putting my five fingers up indicating that I've had enough of her and her sometimey crew. If she wants to pledge allegiance to the mean girls again that's her badd. "The only bitches I see are the ones standing like they're permanently constipated."

104

The crowd now gathered around us snickers as I walk away taking Marcia with me. Poor girl. All she wanted to do was eat her lunch in peace and these heffas had to go and mess up her day.

"Thank you for getting your friends off my back," Marcia says, following me toward the quad in front of the Media Center. This is one of my favorite quiet spots to hang when I can. I should've left campus for lunch, but with gas prices as high as they are there's nowhere I want to go that badly.

"No worries, and they're not my friends," I say, shaking my head at Nellie's behavior. "Well, one of them is, or was but she hasn't been herself lately." I feel bad for my girl. She's acting like a jerk and has no one to blame but herself for the wrath of Jayd when it rains upon her ass.

"This school's so different from my old high school," Marcia says, combing her fingers through her bushy, free-flowing locks. "Everyone was laid back in SD."

"SD?" I ask, unfamiliar with the term.

"Yeah. San Diego. I just moved in with my dad for the first time," she says as the bell rings. Luckily I have Mr. Adewale next period and he'll excuse my tardiness once I explain the situation. "He's not really into clothes and stuff so I take what I can get, you know?"

"Yeah, I know the feeling." I give Marcia a good once over and see the neglect Laura exploited. Mama always says you can spot a motherless child a mile away and she's right: Marcia definitely needs a mother's love. "Here's my number," I say, scribbling down my cell digits on a piece of notebook paper. "Call me if you need anything."

"Thanks, but I'm not a charity case. I'm just doing my time until I can go back home."

If I were her friend I'd dig a little dipper, but I don't want to give

105

Esmeralda any more ammunition to use against me.

"Okay, but just in case," I say, insisting that she take my number.

"Thanks again, Jayd."

"Don't mention it."

There was this beast of a chick named Akeelah who picked on me in elementary school along with my on again/off again friend from around the way, Angela. She was my first frenemy. The first couple of years I took it. Then something happened to me in the fifth grade; something awoke inside of me that changed the game forever. I was no longer afraid of them. There was so much going on with my uncle Donnie's death and other shit that at home that Akeelah no longer incited fear in me. She and Angela used to follow me to the restroom and kick the door open while I was squatting over the toilet—I still have bladder issues due to those incidents.

The last time they bullied me I stood up to Akeelah once and for all. She and Angela cornered me on the playground one afternoon, right between the chain link fence that separated the school from the adjacent graveyard. One minute, me and about ten other girls are taking turns double-dutching and watching the very competitive kickball game across the yard from us. The next, I'm pinned up against the fence being bullied out of my turn.

Akeelah was too tall for any of us to actually get the rope over her head but she'd make us play with her anyway. But that day, in the pleated khaki skirt that my father's mother made for me, I kicked her hard in the shin. Once our fellow jump ropers realized that Akeelah was actually crying, I maneuvered my way through a whole in the fence just big enough for most of us to get through and ran to the other side of the cemetery convinced Akeelah's sidekick, Angela was going to come after me. There was no way Akeelah would make it through the hole without embarrassing herself.

What I never understood was why Angela hung out with Akeelah. It never occurred to me until a couple of years later that maybe Angela was afraid of Akeelah. Akeelah basically forced Angela to be her friend and I guess Angela figured it was better to be Akeelah's friend than to get her ass beat. Smart girl, but I never had that choice. Akeelah hated me from day one, eventhough initially Angela tried to get her to be my friend. I felt sympathy for Angela because I'd known her since kindergarten and considered her to be my best friend at the time. I didn't really blame her for protecting herself, but it did hurt that she didn't choose to ride with me.

If I can help it, Marcia won't be left to the wolves of South Bay High. Besides, after all is said and done, I may need to form a new crew to hang with.

"The unconscious speaks volumes about what it is that you really want, and who."
-Jeremy
Drama High, volume 12: Pushin'

~ 10 ~
SWEPT UP

Compared to the lunchtime sideshow, the rest of my Monday was pretty uneventful. Netta's sisters are holding down the shop so that she can tend to Mama's daily needs. I'm just glad she's awake. I miss her being just a phone call or a thought away.

"Mama, what really happened between you and Mrs. Esop?" I ask, passing her the thick manila envelope Nigel gave me during fifth period. She needs to take a look at the legal documents before I deliver them to Mrs. Carmichael for the final seal of approval. Even on Mama's worst day she can outwit Mrs. Esop's vindictive antics.

The last time I saw Nigel's mom she was in pretty bad shape. Her daughter, Natasia, is getting married to her girlfriend this spring and Mrs. Esop's not happy about it to say the least. I hope his mom's feeling better now that Nigel's back home. Even if I feel for Mrs. Esop in a small way, all of the drama that she's experiencing she really brought on herself. She should've known better than to come after me for not finishing the damned debutante ball, and through Mama nonetheless.

"Teresa and I were good friends at one time," Mama says, placing the envelope on Dr. Whitmore's desk. She's made herself right at home in the quaint space. "We met at Xavier our freshman year in college. She was very driven and wanted so badly to marry an athlete, which is exactly what she ended up doing."

"You have to admire her tenacity," I say, taking a seat on the futon. The look Mama shoots me immediately shuts me up. After all, this is her story and giving props to the antagonist isn't wise.

"Teresa pledged Alpha Gamma Rho our freshman year and I pledged sophomore year. Because we were already friends I thought it would be natural for us to become sorors—or sisters—in the sorority. After all, I am my mother's only child and liked the idea of being in an organization that endorsed sisterhood among black women. But I had no idea that I would have to sell my soul to do it."

"Mmmhmmm," Netta says, sweeping the floor. "And she almost lost her best friend and soul sister in the process."

"Oh Netta, are you ever going to let me live that down?" Mama says, smiling at her friend.

"Hell no, Lynn Mae. Never, not ever!" Netta can be so silly sometimes.

Mama cuts her eyes at Netta, and Netta returns the favor.

"As time passed I forgot about that experience as best I could," Mama continues. "I left college without graduating, got married, moved to Compton with your grandfather and started our family. It wasn't until I ran into Teresa at the Lakewood Mall that I knew she was living here, too. Her husband's family lived in Compton until The Clippers drafted him first, then The Lakers years later, which is when they moved to Lafayette Square." Mama reclaims the envelope and removes its contents. "What Teresa won't tell anyone is that she couldn't initially conceive a child, and that's when she came to me. I helped her with both of her pregnancies."

"What?" I say, surprised by Mama's truth telling. "No wonder she's overly invested in both Nigel and Natasia's lives." I seriously

109

doubt that her children know of my grandmother's history with their mother.

"Precisely, Jayd. That woman is a mother hen times ten. I don't blame her for being involved in her children's lives, but she's involved to the point of controlling and that means that eventually they'll resent her very presence."

"They already do," I say, again recalling my last visit to the Esop compound. "Natasia and her fiancé announced their engagement to Mrs. Esop who refuses to accept the fact that her daughter's a proud lesbian in love."

"The emotion of love is the only constant in a world full of change, and we all better get it whenever and wherever we can, damn what others may think," Netta says, breaking it down. "Love is active; love is a constant test in devotion, your pain threshold, and perseverance. You can love a person, a calling, a talent, a pet. As long as you love truly you'll receive love in return."

Netta always gives me food for thought. I feel like I love hard but rarely receive the same love in return.

"Teresa's never liked anything too different," Mama says, tossing the papers back down on the desk. "She never accepted that we each represent different paths of the Creator, and so do her children. Some people call them attributes, saints, or Orishas as we do, and they all have life to give. But we can become distracted, be lead astray from our divine paths, and that's where the drama begins."

"I hear that," I chime in.

Netta and Mama both laugh at my testimony. They of all people know how much drama I have in my life at any given time.

"Before you know it, little Jayd, one side of Legba takes over and all hell breaks loose. It can happen time and time again until you learn your lesson," Netta says.

Mama nods in affirmation. "The power is in the choices you make and when you make them. For example, it was all right for me to have more than one boyfriend in college—that was part of my Oshune path. Erzulie Freda is her more playful side, but that side of our mother doesn't bode well for a married woman. But unlike Teresa, I don't believe in giving up all life's joy once we take on adulthood rites."

"That Teresa's always been a piece of work," Netta says, tying a red band around the wooden and straw broom she just constructed. "I still don't see how you were ever friends with her."

"It's all water under the bridge now," Mama says, sprinkling water on the floor where Netta's sweeping. "I feel sorry for her. Teresa's a proud woman and that pride is what keeps her from enjoying the fullness of life, I don't care how much money she has."

Uh oh, I feel a spirit lesson coming on.

"Alafia, ladies," Mr. Adewale says, entering the office. "The doctor's out back working and says he'll be inside with your dinner soon, Iyalosha."

Damn, Mama's got it made in the shade staying here. She might as well be on vacation. I've taken on her clients at home, the boys and Daddy are on their own when it comes to housework, and Netta's sisters are holding down the shop, leaving Mama to basically chill until this madness with Esmeralda passes.

"Thank you, Ogunlabi," Mama says, kissing him on the cheek. "Did you bring your broom?"

"I did," he says, pulling out a short broom similar to the one Netta's using. "It's already dressed."

111

"Excellent," Mama says, taking it from him and whipping it around in the air. "Ogun always makes the best tools."

"Yes he does," Netta agrees. "Come on over here, iyawo. It's time for your next lesson."

I dutifully obey already knowing the drill.

"It's time for you to start playing with voodoo dolls and doing broom work, little miss," Netta says, holding up Mama's doll and brushing it with her broom.

I've always been afraid of the broom closet at Mama's house and rarely swept as a result, leaving that task to my cousin Jay. When I was little I could hear mice burrowing through it to get inside of the kitchen. It was always a mess, packed with old grocery bags, brooms, mops and anything else my uncles decided to put in there. But the one in the spirit room is immaculately kept.

"I'm going to teach you how to use brooms to sweep away our enemies, and instead sweep up some good energy by properly dressing them with your ashe," Netta says, taking out a bunch of straw, twine and other goodies from her large bag.

"Listen carefully, Jayd," Mama says, taking a seat next to me. "This is how we're going to defeat Esmeralda and Rousseau once and for all."

"I'm down with that," I say, preparing for a long evening. I take out my spirit notebook ready to take notes.

"As you know, part of my lineage's gifts are doing hair," Netta says, instinctively fixing a wayward strand on Mama's head. "But we actually deal with anything involving all types of hair, including old brooms made from horse hair and straw."

"There's always more work to do," I say, jokingly but not really. It

112

seems that every hour of every day calls for work of some sort.

"Jayd, as my favorite author Zora Neale Hurston once said, black women are the mules of the world," Mama says, looking exhausted. "Get used to working all day, every day because like it or not, this work right here is for the rest of your life."

"You'd better enjoy the work you choose to do, Jayd," Mr. Adewale says, adding his three cents. "Thus the college applications."

I picked the wrong audience to express my feelings to in regards to working, I see. There's no sympathy for a sister up in here.

"Okay, Jayd," Netta says, handing me a wooden stick, a handful of straw and some twine. "I want you to try fixing your own broom with your hair first. See yourself as weaving in all of the good things you want for yourself. Protection, power, money, love just to name a few: All the good that life has to offer."

I pull out a few strands from my ponytail and begin weaving them together with the straw. Mr. Adewale hands me more. I look at Mama's voodoo doll and think about how much I want to help protect my grandmother from our enemies. As I envision all of the things I want to bring into my life, Maman's powers take over my site. I'm instantly caught up in the rapture of the vision.

I'm inside of the same beauty shop that I was in during my last vision as Mama, but instead of being my grandmother this time I'm just a witness to more of the abuse Maman endured at the hands of her husband, Jean Paul.

"I will kill you if it's the last thing I do," Maman says, holding on tightly to her infant daughter. I should be used to seeing Mama as a baby but it freaks me out every time.

"Your wish is my command, ma chere," Jean Paul says, attempting

113

to rise from the floor where my great-grandmother has him virtually paralyzed through her site. His head is pulsating from her hold on him but he's got one more trick up his sleeve.

"Jean Paul, no!" Maman screams.

He pulls out a broom and sweeps it toward her. "Damn you to hell, Marie! You'll never live without me! Never!"

Refusing to let go of her hold on him, Maman Marie's stare becomes more intense. Baby Mama cries in agony as if she senses that something is terribly wrong with her mother. The more Jean Paul squirms in pain, the more intense Maman's green eyes glow.

"I'd rather become an ancestor than remain your wife." Her eyes tear up with water first, and then it changes to blood. The crimson tears drip onto Mama's forehead as if she's being baptized.

Jean Paul can't take it anymore. He drops the broom and slumps over, takes his final breath, and Maman's life with it.

"Maman!" I scream out in horror. It took all of her life force to kill her husband and keep her baby safe from his evil ways. She paid the ultimate sacrifice to put her husband's reign of terror in New Orleans to an end.

"Jayd, snap out of it!" I can hear Mama say into my ear, but just like when she was in her dream state I'm not going to wake up until it's over.

Baby Mama's hysterical as Maman falls to the ground across from her husband's body. She drops Mama who luckily lands on her padded bottom. Maman's stream of tears have turned into a river of blood. I run over to Maman and kneel down beside her. I can't stop crying as I look my great-grandmother in the eye. Mama reaches up to me and I hold her tightly crying with them both.

114

"Remember, Jayd. Our vision is our life. Without it, we become the *walking dead.*" Maman grabs my face and forces me closer. "Vision *equals life, Jayd. Never loose your site.*" Maman's green glow takes over her entire body. I can't move or let go of Mama who's mystified by her mother's transformation from flesh to total spirit. "You have all of me, my *daughters. Now, go and cast out your enemies as I did with mine!*"

The vision switches to Esmeralda in her kitchen: It looks like current day. She's busy making voodoo dolls with both her clients' and victims' hair. There's also a clear vile on the counter with what looks like blood in it marked 'Lynn Mae'. That must be Mama's blood from the night she was attacked.

"*Esmeralda,*" I say.

She can't hear me, but I can tell by Netta's shouting that I'm speaking aloud.

I finally wake up to find myself kneeling on the floor near the front door.

"Baby, are you okay?" Mama asks, helping me to my feet.

"Yeah, I think so. But I've got a wicked headache." I rub my temples first, then my eyes, which also feel a little off.

"Jayd, your eyes," Netta says with her mouth wide open.

Mr. Adewale drops his broom.

What are they all staring at?

Mama stares at me, amazed. She hands me a mirror and I can't believe my eyes, either.

"My eyes...they're green," I say, pulling at my lids to make sure they're mine. When I was a little girl I used to pray to have green eyes like all of the other women in my lineage. Eventually, I grew to love my brown eyes, but now that I'm rocking the jade ones I love it. They feel

115

so powerful, and so good.

"Yes, I can see that," Mama says. She takes me by the chin and turns my face from one side to the other. "You have my mother's eyes," she says, staring at me like I stole something.

"Maman led my vision. At the very end she grabbed my face, kinda like you're doing now, and forced me to stare into her eyes." I back away from my grandmother who looks confused and dare I say, angry. "It must've been right before she died," I say, instantly seeing that my words have unintentionally hurt my grandmother. I can't help but feel like I've betrayed her in some way even if it wasn't my fault.

"I have to talk to the doctor," Mama says, walking toward the back door. "It's too soon for you to carry all of that power."

Netta and Mr. Adewale look at me unsure of how to handle the situation. They can feel my grandmother's heat, too.

"Don't worry, baby," Netta says, embracing me. "It's going to be okay. Dr. Whitmore will figure out what's going on."

I accept the hug and the wisdom, but we both know that things are far from okay. Mama's used to being in control and I can only imagine how crazy this situation must be driving her. I hope she knows that I would never do anything to intentionally hurt her. Whatever the reason Maman saw fit to give me her sight, I'm positive it's only temporary until our work with Rousseau and Esmeralda is done. And I hate to say it, but ultimately Maman is the head priestess in charge. If this is the way it has to be, then we all need to bow down in order to defeat our enemies sooner rather than later.

"Jayd's become an ornery little wench, hasn't she Lynn Mae?"
-Daddy
Drama High, volume 11: Cold As Ice

~11~
H.P.I.C.

Mama said that I had to go back into whites and sleep in the spirit room until my eyes return to normal. Apparently with the green vision comes lofty aspirations, or so the spirit book says. Eventhough I miss the solitude of my mom's apartment, Mama needs me nearby for her own peace of mind and for me to keep things in check with her clients. I also need the protection of my uncles and their notoriously crazy behavior to keep these fools around here from attacking me even more than they already are. I don't know anyone in Inglewood except my mom's neighbors and they can't help me when it comes to Rousseau and Esmeralda.

After Monday's near-fight between Nellie, Marcia and myself, I decided to take the high road and not speak to Nellie until she comes to her senses. I also tried talking to Mickey, but now that her man is out on probation she's been preoccupied with her family planning, even at the expense of her school attendance. There are only three more days left in the school week and she hasn't bothered to show up at all.

"Jayd, I need some toilet paper," Bryan yells through the cracked bathroom door. There are many things I haven't missed about living here and dealing with funky ass dudes is the main one.

"And some incense." I reach into the hall closet, pull out a roll and toss it to him.

"I got your incense," Bryan says, reclosing the door.

In addition to working with Mama's regulars, I've also taken on a few school clients of my own, making voodoo love charms, protection potions and a few incantations to help with self-confidence. I made one for Marcia and hopes she utilizes it immediately. The vultures have swooned in on her as easy prey. The sooner she rectifies that shit the better her school year will be. Mama warned me about taking on other people's problems and I hear her, but I still feel like I should do something to help those who desperately need it.

"I feel ten pounds lighter, niecey," Bryan says as he exits the bathroom and closes the door behind him. He walks across the hall into Mama's room and plops down on the foot of my bed. We all miss Mama's presence in the household.

"Way too much info, Unc," I say, kicking him in the thigh.

"Here. Get busy," Bryan says, tossing me a stack of coupons while he stacks the rest. We start clipping for Daddy's usual shopping trip in the morning.

"I'm busy, or haven't you noticed the pile of books on my lap?" I've missed hanging out with my Uncle Bryan and from the looks of it he's missed me, too.

"I know you can do two things at once, just like Kimmy Cakes can handle me and her baby-daddy," he says, turning up the volume on Keeping Up With the Kardashians. He's tripping if he thinks I'm about to watch this madness.

"Bryan, I know your conscious ass isn't feeling that trick," I say, attempting to rescue the remote to no avail. Bryan's bigger, stronger, and faster than me.

As we continue clipping and chatting about silly shit on television, Jay walks in with a chip on his shoulder.

"Jayd, why did you tell Mr. Baxter that I didn't graduate from high

118

school?" he says with his hands on his hips. Someone needs to tell him that's not an attractive quality.

"Because you didn't, fool." Why is he sweating me? It came up in conversation when our neighbor across the street asked how the family was doing. After helping me with Mama's episode a couple of weeks ago they have been extra inquisitive.

"I did graduate by taking the GED. I just didn't walk. Stop telling people all my business, Jayd, especially when you don't know what the hell you're talking about." Jay storms out of our grandmother's room and into the neighboring room he, Bryan and Daddy share.

"Damn, Jay. You act like you left high school to become a secret agent or something," I yell out of the opened door. "You got promoted to manager at Costco. Big deal." I know that was a bit harsh but he's been smelling himself big time ever since he started making more money than he ever has in his life. Hell, he makes more money than any of our uncles have ever made. I am proud of him, but I still think he's going about his newfound career the wrong way. In my opinion, he still needs to go to college.

"Just because you got to go to a rich, white high school and take all AP classes doesn't mean that's what we're all supposed to do, Jayd," he yells back. "Just shut up when your mouth begins to form my name if you aren't speaking directly to me." Jay slams the bedroom door and turns up his radio.

"Damn, what's eating him?" I ask Bryan, who's as shocked by Jay's response as I am.

"He's been out of sorts lately," Bryan says, changing the channel. "I think it's the long hours. I told him a promotion ain't always a good thing."

119

My phone rings with another call from Keenan. He isn't happy about my temporary relocation and thinks I've been avoiding him. He's gotten a little arrogant about my unavailable status to the point of being slightly controlling and it's turning me off. I push ignore on my cell and toss the phone down. It rings again, this time with a call from Jeremy.

"Hello," I answer, excited to hear from him outside of school even if we're not supposed to be talking.

"Peace, Lady J." Just the sound of his voice makes me melt inside. "I was just thinking about the last time I played a really good game of chess and you came to mind, of course."

If he could see my smile through the phone he'd know how much I still care about him and miss us. "Aching for an ass whipping, I see."

"Language, young lady," Bryan says, pinching my left big toe.

I playfully kick Bryan in the back and step into the dining room for more privacy.

"I can see that humility escapes you." I can hear Jeremy's smile through the phone. "But seriously, Jayd. I miss my friend."

"And I miss mine." To hell with being coy. There's just something about Jeremy that I can't shake, damn the pretenses.

"Can we see each other, outside of school? Look Jayd, I know you're seeing somebody new," Jeremy begins.

"And you're seeing Cameron," I say, reminding him of the real issue between us. Keenan would've never had space to move in if Jeremy and me were still together and rolling hard like we used to.

"No. Cameron's seeing me. My eyes never left you, Jayd. I hope you know that."

"I do, Jeremy," I say, feeling his pain.

120

Before I can confess all my love to my ex, one of Esmeralda's crows lands on the porch railing eavesdropping for it's master, no doubt. My eyes begin to glow as I catch the bird's beady eyes by surprise and lock onto them.

"Jayd, are you there?" Jeremy asks. I would love to get lost on the phone with my ex but duty calls.

"Jeremy, I have to go. Can we continue this conversation later?" I ask without letting go of my visual hold on the bird.

"Of course."

I hang up my phone and step out onto the porch. The bird looks paralyzed as Maman's powers take over. "I want you to bring me locks of Esmeralda and Rousseau's hair. Now!" I command, knowing that Maman's in my head even if I can't hear her. Esmeralda needs to know that just because Mama's not here that doesn't mean that she automatically became the head priestess in charge.

"Jayd, I need you to learn how to part destinies into the dolls' heads through braiding their hair," Maman says into my head. I guess now that I've got her eyes she's got free range to my thoughts, just like her daughter and granddaughter do. *"Look it up in the spirit book and I'll explain in detail later. Go to the spirit room after the bird returns with the hair."*

Oh hell. Here we go. I guess my night of studying and calling Jeremy back is a wrap. As always, spirit work trumps all else. I'm still glad he called. Once this is all over with Esmeralda I'll find a way to get Cameron off Jeremy's ass.

Surprisingly I wasn't late for school this morning although I had a long night. Jeremy cornered me in the library this morning before the

121

first bell rang. He didn't speak to me and I didn't say a word to him, either. He simply put my face in his hands, bent down and kissed me softly. All of our emotions seemed to rise to our lips, and we stayed that way until the final bell rang. I've been thinking about that kiss all morning and more importantly, how Cameron would react if she found out about it. I have no doubt that she'd rather see Jeremy back on lock down than with me any day.

Jeremy proposed that we see each other in secret. He claims his life is dull without me in it and I feel the same way. With my entire crew tripping, having Jeremy in my life provides a sort of normalcy that I need right now. I didn't necessarily agree to his suggestion but I am considering it. Besides, keeping our relationship a secret has its benefits when it comes to Esmeralda's conniving ways as well.

"Anybody got some lotion?" Shae asks, interrupting the afternoon announcements. She's so hood it should be a crime.

Marcia wants to laugh out loud at the ghetto intrusion but covers her smile. What's that all about?

"Here," Misty says, passing Shae some cocoa butter lotion. Her bag looks like a beauty supply rather than a student's tool for carrying books.

"Ladies, please. The announcements are on," Mr. Adewale says, checking the time. He usually has us after lunch not before, and everyone's pretty antsy.

The school schedule is special today, with each class shortened by fifteen minutes due to our morning assembly. Who made the final cut for homecoming court, the student council candidates, and when the class rings and yearbook packages will go on sale are included in the extra intrusion.

122

"Damn it. I missed the announcements for Maggie's nomination," I say, gathering my things. Neither Mickey nor Nellie decided to show up for class today. It must be nice to pick and choose when you want to come to school.

Misty glares at me and then rolls her blue eyes to Mr. Adewale's back. She was the first person to notice my new eye color. Like everyone else, Misty took them for contact lenses. I thought she'd know better, having gone through a similar transformation during her initiation into Esmeralda's house, but I guess she's as stupid as her godmother when it comes to the depth of our powers.

"No worries, girl. You know Maggie got this," Chase says, putting his cap back on. The bells about to ring and I'm starving. Maybe he'll be nice and treat a sistah to lunch off campus today.

"Don't forget your homework. And for those of you participating in the debate, don't forget to continue with your research," Mr. Adewale says, dismissing class.

As I join the line of students making their way toward the lunch quad, a white girl pulls off her ponytail holder and releases her hair across my face. This is the type of shit that makes me want to cut a chick's hair off. And with my newfound knowledge of brooms and dolls, she'd best be careful.

"So what's for lunch, big bro?" I ask, playfully holding Chase's hand. "It's been a minute since I had some good pizza."

"You know I got you," Chase says, ushering me toward the parking lot. "I already had plans but you're welcomed to join us, if you don't mind." Chase disarms his alarm on the classic Nova where Jeremy's waiting for his best friend.

"I don't mind at all." Before I can get too happy about the free lunch and good company, the bitch of the year and her crew cut our reunion short.

"Going somewhere?" Cameron asks, with Laura and the rest of their girls in tow.

It's times like this that I miss having a strong female crew. With the right broads on my side, heffas like Cameron would never feel free to step up to me no matter the situation.

Jeremy sighs. "We're just grabbing a bite to eat, Cameron."

"Excellent. Where to?" Cameron wraps her arms around Jeremy's waist and kisses his arm, inciting a heat in me that I don't recognize.

"Actually, it was just me and Chase going," Jeremy says, separating himself from his leach.

"And Jayd," Chase says, looking at Jeremy. He did forget to mention me, and it was so nice of my play brother to check his friend on my behalf. "I invited her, too. So if you don't mind, time's a wasting," Chase says, starting the car via remote control.

Laura's eyes grow wide with excitement at the hum of the powerful engine. I know how she feels. There's nothing like Chase's ride to bring a smile to a girl's face.

"Well, if she's going then I'm definitely going," Cameron says, reclaiming Jeremy like he's property instead of a person.

"Damn, you're one hungry bitch," I say to Cameron before I can second-guess my actions. I'm done holding my tongue around this trick.

"Nice eyes, Jayd. Did you buy them at the Dollar Store?" Cameron says, attempting to throw salt, but she has no idea how to box with a champion.

"Thanks, Cameron. Want to see what they can do?" I narrow my eyes and contemplate which of the powers in my arsenal to hit her with first.

Cameron lets go of Jeremy and steps in my face. I wish she'd throw a punch because I'd certainly return the favor.

"You may have everyone else around here convinced they should be afraid of you because you're some kind of witch or something, but I'm not afraid of you, Jayd. Bring it on!"

"Cameron, go sit down somewhere before you get hurt. Seriously," Chase says, looking at his platinum Rolex. "It's time to go, y'all."

"The hell it is. Jeremy, you're coming with me," Cameron says, pointing to her convertible BMW parked on the other side of the lot.

"I told you, I already have plans." Jeremy opens the passenger door and nods to Chase who opens the driver's side door. He pushes the lever and the seat bends forward for me to get in the back.

"Aren't you forgetting our agreement?" Cameron says, tapping on her blinged-out iPhone case. I hope she breaks her freshly manicured nails on it.

"Damn, Cameron. Give it a rest," Chase says, wiping the sweat from his brow. "You give ball and chain a whole new meaning."

"And it's too hot out here for this shit. I'll catch you later, Cameron. Cool?" Jeremy says, trying to appease the bitch, but she's way out of pocket this afternoon. Jeremy's becoming more unattractive every second he let's this heffa punk him.

My eyes start to burn I'm so pissed. "Cameron, step back before you go too far."

Cameron looks as if she's considering my words but then she

steps closer, almost touching me nose to nose. "Jeremy's mine, Jayd. Just stay out of my damned way!"

"No, Cameron. He's not. And anyone can tell that he doesn't want to be with you."

"But I have him now, and that's all that matters," Cameron says, sounding more insane the louder she yells. Even her girls look tired of her rampage.

"Obviously you don't have him, you psychotic wench. If you did, why is he still trying to get with me on the low?"

"What is she talking about, Jeremy?" Cameron screams. "I told you I would not tolerate any indiscretions, ever!"

Other students anxious to get off campus look at the scene and keep stepping. I wish I could walk away, too.

"But you will tolerate being with a man who hates you," I say, bringing her back to reality with the rest of us. This trick is really off her rocker. "How pathetic can you be?"

Cameron stares at me and I stare right back. She looks at me so intensely that my head gets hot and my eyes begin to burn. Before I can stop her, Cameron lunges toward me, slapping me to the ground.

"Oh shit!" Chase says. He moves out of the way, knowing I can handle myself.

"Get off of me!" I scream, snatching Cameron's long, brown hair and forcing her head back into an unnatural position. I look into her eyes and attempt to calm her down with my mom's sight but it's no use. Cameron's literally too hot for me to handle.

"Not until you get off my man!" Cameron attempts to scratch my face but I dodge the assault, still controlling her head. She then kicks one of her Dolce and Gabana sandals at me, hitting me in the arm.

"That's it!" I say, standing. The whole turning the other cheek thing is good in theory but it's not working for me in this moment. I pull Cameron up to her feet and put her in a headlock like my uncles used to do to me when we would play fight. It wasn't fun to me when I was little, but now that I'm older I see the benefit in the unwelcomed entrapment.

"Hey, what's going on here?" the security guards call out, entering the gated lot. "Let her go!"

Ah hell, now I know I'm in for it. I do as I'm told and stand my ground. I didn't do anything wrong but I know I'm still going to go down for this shit.

"This chick just went crazy on my homegirl," Chase says, coming to my defense. "We just wanted to get some lunch."

Jeremy doesn't move or speak up. What the hell?

"That's not true!" Laura screams at Chase. "This girl attacked my friend."

"Laura, shut the hell up with your lying ass," I say as calmly as I can. "Officers, I can explain," I say, but Tweedledee and Tweedledum aren't interested in the truth.

"Save it for the principal," the biggest one says. "Let's go, ladies."

"Focus your energy in the right direction and really make a difference."
-Ms. Toni
Drama High, volume 2: Second Chance

~12~
GOOD INTENTIONS

Because of Cameron's little temper tantrum and Laura's lying on Wednesday, the three of us were placed on in-house suspension all day yesterday. Once I explained my side of the story to Mr. Adewale and Ms. Toni they vouched for me with the principal, and so did Chase. You'd think the administration would let me go and apologize for not believing me, but instead I have to sit through this damned meeting with Cameron, Laura and their mothers. I can't believe I was involved in yet another fight over a boy who didn't even come to my defense like he should've. Will I ever get too old for this drama?

"Nope, so learn to keep your mouth shut and just deal with it, baby," my mom says, lending me her twisted support.

"Thanks mom, but I've got this," I think back. Her mental hijacking is actually a welcomed distraction to the bull going on around me. What a waste of a perfectly good Friday morning.

"When my daughter arrives on campus in the morning I expect you to do your job, John, and that includes protecting her from your bussed in students," Cameron's mom says, making it clear why my presence was requested even though I've been cleared of any wrongdoing. "I shouldn't have to do a damned thing when she comes home from school but ask her how her day was." Cameron's mom is a piece of work. No wonder her daughter's such a spoiled brat.

"I agree with Catherine," Laura's mom says. "I've never been so humiliated in all my life, John."

Somehow I truly doubt that. Whether Mindy knows about it or not, her daughter's done much worse.

"It wasn't our intention to make you uncomfortable," Mr. Adelizi says.

"Mindy, you know I didn't want to have to do this," Principal Shepherd says, on a first name basis with their parents. I don't even think he knows my parents exist, which is just fine with me.

"But you did. You know our girls would never start a fight. They come from a good home and have no need to resort to violence, unless provoked."

Mindy and Catherine look at me hard as if the mere suggestion that their debutantes couldn't possibly attack a little hoodrat like me will change the facts. Too bad it happened in the parking lot where the video surveillance provided indisputable evidence.

"Mindy, Catherine, unfortunately that wasn't the case," Principal Shepherd says, cuing the recording on his wide screen television.

We all watch the incident in real time with audio included. I'm the only one in the room smiling.

"Well, I think Cameron's learned her lesson from this unfortunate occurrence," Catherine says. "My daughter won't respond like that to obvious provocation again."

"What provocation?" I ask, tired of being unfairly accused. "All I wanted to do was eat lunch until Cameron and Laura prevented me from doing so."

"If I may," Mr. Adelizi interjects. If this was a meeting for us regular students the special circumstances counselor would be present, not our senior guidance counselor. "I think it's a good idea to put this all into perspective before it continues to escalate, and no one wants that."

"Agreed," Principal Shepherd says, leaning back in his leather chair.

"What do you want to do after high school, Laura?" Mr. Adelizi asks, attempting to provide guidance when what Laura really needs is a good ass whipping from my grandmother. That'll straighten her out.

"Marry Reid and raise our children."

She sounds just like Cameron's delusional ass, except I think this trick is really going to make it happen. Her mother's beaming with pride. I guess the mad apple doesn't fall too far from the crazy tree.

"Well," Mr. Adelizi says, shifting uncomfortably in his seat. "Whatever your post high school goals are, lying isn't going to help any of them." At least one person here is on my side, sort of.

Laura begins to protest but realizes it's in vain. She's busted and we all know it.

"And, Cameron. I must say that I'm very disappointed in your behavior. What possessed you to attack Jayd?"

Cameron's mother sighs with impatience. "I don't see the point of this continued grilling, John. The girls served their time yesterday."

Before the principal can answer Mr. Adelizi responds. "The point is, Mrs. Preston, that Cameron's behavior is grounds for expulsion." Mr. Adelizi points to the school code of conduct on the wall behind him.

Finally, someone lays down the law on this trick. If it were me in the hot seat I'd already be kicked out of South Bay High.

"The girls said they were sorry for the misunderstanding," Laura's mom says, coming to Cameron's defense. "Isn't that enough?"

"No, it isn't," I say, standing up for myself. "I missed a day and a half of classes because of Cameron's actions and had to serve in-house suspension when I did nothing wrong."

"Jayd, please," Mr. Adelizi begins, but he knows I'm right.

"We're not little kids anymore," I continue. Even Principal John appears to be listening. "And I for one am tired of being treated like a criminal when I'm the victim here in more ways than one."

"What do you mean by that, Jayd?" Mr. Adelizi asks, still in counseling mode.

Cameron's entire demeanor changes from a badass young woman to a helpless child at the mere insinuation of the real reason we're all in this predicament. I've held my tongue long enough trying to protect Jeremy. He didn't even know how to have my back when the time came: To hell with him and his ball and chain, as Chase calls her.

"Cameron's been blackmailing my ex boyfriend, Jeremy, to be her boyfriend," I say, feeling the weight of deception lift from my shoulders. "And he doesn't want to be with her. Jeremy wants to be back with me and that's why Cameron attacked me. Can I go now?"

"That's simply not true!" Cameron's mom screams at the top of her lungs. "She's lying! Look at her. What boy in his right mind would choose her over my daughter?"

Laura's mom shakes her head in agreement. "Cameron's perfect! Just like Laura."

The term 'hoe sit down' was made for moments like this, but I can't disrespect my elders no matter how foul they may be.

"If you don't believe me check her fancy phone," I say, pointing at the sparkly device permanently glued to the girl's right hand. "Cameron has the video that broke us up saved on her cell. She's been holding it over Jeremy's head as collateral to get her way for months, and I'm done."

I stand up and wait for permission to leave. It finally comes via Mr. Adelizi.

"I'll take it from here, Jayd. And we're sorry you had to endure this type of injustice," Mr. Adelizi says. He looks at the principal who looks stuck between a rock and me.

"We'll make sure this doesn't go on your permanent record and that your teachers are fully aware of the situation," Mr. Shepherd says. He looks down at the papers on his desk and sighs heavily.

I smile victoriously at my enemies and leave the office. I feel better already. If there's a way to get that same type of vindication when it comes to how Mrs. Bennett constantly persecutes my ass I need to find it.

"Jayd, I've been looking everywhere for you," Mickey says, walking me down in the main hall. I only have a few minutes to get to English class and no time for her latest emergency.

"What is it, Mickey? I've had a rough morning." I slam my locker door shut and head toward the Language Arts corridor.

Mickey pulls a braid out of her purse and waves it in my face. "My hair came out in second period. Can you please put it back in for me?"

"Mickey, you know I don't deal with anything fake," I say, laughing at her dilemma. Only she would ask me to stop what I'm doing to help her out when she hasn't spoken more than two words to me in weeks.

"Really? Have you looked in the mirror lately?" she says, referring to my eye color.

Rather than tell her the unbelievable truth, I snatch the braid out of her hand and lead her toward my class. I glance inside hoping Mrs. Bennett doesn't see me and notice that we have a substitute today. There is a God, and she has a little mercy on me. This day just keeps getting better and better.

"Bend down," I say, setting my book bag and purse down by the front door. Most of the other students are in class talking and sitting in the wrong seats, clearly taking advantage of the sub.

"Thank you so much," Mickey says, tilting her head forward so that I can reach the back of her head. "I would've done it myself but I can't get a good grip in the back."

"You can't get a good grip because your hair is thinning from you stressing it out," I say, observing her crown. "How did this happen anyway? It looks like it was snatched out."

The sub looks out the door and notices me working. Like most of the other white folks up here, she doesn't know what to say and steps back inside.

"It was an accident," Mickey says, pressing her index finger at the root of the braid to keep it from pulling out the rest of her hair. "I was in the girl's bathroom and it got caught in one of the stall doors. That shit hurt like hell."

"You've got to be more careful," I say, finishing up the braid. The bell starts to ring and I braid faster, not wanting to be marked tardy even if I am standing in the doorway.

"Thank God Misty was there to help me get untangled. Not that I like the trick or anything, but she did help me out."

"Misty helped you?" I ask, suspicious of the good deed. "Are you sure she didn't trap your braids in the door intentionally?"

"Jayd, you're so paranoid about everything," Mickey says, feeling the braid reinforced against her scalp. It looks better than the rest of her braids, that's for sure. "You should go to that college party tonight. You need to loosen up."

"Honestly I forgot all about it." Keenan wanted me to make an appearance as his date and I turned him down. Maybe I should reconsider. I need to let my hair down and enjoy life a little.

"Well, think about it. Later," Mickey says, strolling to class.

If she only knew what was going on in my world Mickey wouldn't dare ask me to attend any kind of party. I'm surprised she's considering going. With Nigel being the top football recruit for UCLA next fall, I'm sure he's going to be there. Come to think of it, most of my dilapidated crew should be in attendance, including Rah. All rational signs say don't go, but something about my bright vision is telling me to check it out. With all of my closest friends in one place something bad is bound to happen, and it may be just the time for me to cast a protection spell to cover us all.

"You should come to the party, Jayd," Nigel says, turning the corner late to his own class.

"What, are you spying on me now?" I say, giving him a quick hug.

"Not you," he says, as serious as a heart attack. Mickey's not the only one who can scheme to get what she wants. "It'll be fun, Jayd. What's wrong with that?"

Nigel's right. I need to blow off some steam, and the party will give me and Keenan a chance to hang. I've been neglecting him for far too long.

"Okay, I'll go."

~ 1 3 ~
THE TALK

It was the longest Friday ever. I tried to hunt down Misty and grill
her about her good deed but she was nowhere to be found. Mickey also
disappeared after lunch off to God only knows where. With any luck
everyone I need to lay eyes on will appear at tonight's festivities. I took
time to look up an incantation that should throw a much needed
protection blanket over me and my crew.

The plan is to meet at Chase's house and then he'll drive me and
Nigel to the party in Westwood, truly a city unto itself. Keenan gave me
a tour of UCLA's sovereign town and I was in awe of the wealth
surrounding the university campus. As much as Nigel wants to front like
he's not, I know he's equally impressed, especially with the illegal
perks that come with his station. Chase is Nigel's top champion for
accepting gifts from all of the schools interested in Nigel, which is a
slippery slope but neither of them will listen to reason. They just want to
have fun and enjoy the moment.

*"Maybe you should take notes from your friends and stop trying to
be the mama all the damned time,"* my mom chimes in. I'm running late
as it is and don't need her mental harassment right now, but I have no
choice. She can jump in and out of my mind at will, even when we're
standing in the same room.

"Mom, you can just talk to me, you know," I say, eyeing my
understated outfit in her floor-length mirrored closet doors. Although
most of her wardrobe is at her fiancé's house, she leaves some pieces

here just in case, and I'm grateful for it. Being restricted to wearing white underneath everything severely limits my wardrobe options.

"You think I don't know what I can and cannot do?" My mom can be so much to handle sometimes and she knows it. "All I'm saying is that you have the rest of your life to work, Jayd. Have some fun without attaching work to it while you can, because after high school, shit gets real."

"I'm not braiding anyone's head tonight," I say, running my fingers through my wavy tresses. I took my cornrows out a little while ago and decided to just let my hair be. It feels good.

My mom glares at me with that look that says, "You know what I'm talking about, young lady." Daddy gave it to her and me, and now she's throwing it around.

"Mom, you do realize that Mama's not safe and neither am I or my friends as long as Esmeralda's spell is in effect?"

"That type of bull right there is why I got out when I did," my mom mutters under her breath. She always reminds me of how much better her life is because she gave up her sight after she unwisely left Mama's house when she was a teenager.

"In hindsight, do you really think that was the best way to go? You forget I lived it," I say, recalling one of my worst sleepwalking experiences ever. Esmeralda stripping my mom's power was more painful than anything I've ever experienced, including Mickey's labor pains. My mom's right; it's not easy living with our gifts but I can't imagine being any other way.

"I didn't forget a damned thing, Jayd, including the hell that heffa put me through." We both shiver at the thought of Esmeralda. "But she didn't have Rousseau back then. Esmeralda's more powerful than I ever imagined she could be, and she's going after my mother and my daughter. I hate to admit it, but I'm scared that we may not win this battle, Jayd." My mom sits at the foot of her bed and I join her. I've never seen my mother this worried before.

I put my left arm around her narrow frame as she rests her head on my shoulder. "That's exactly why I have to stay on my game, mom. In this moment, I'm the only one who can do the work necessary to check Esmeralda and hopefully send Rousseau back to whatever hellhole he crept out of."

"I want you to be seventeen, Jayd," my mom says, her emerald eyes tearing up. "Take a break from the spirit studies and voodoo dolls and whatnot. Be a teenager, go to a party and have some fun. Meet some other boys besides Keenan the player."

I begin to protest but it would be in vain. My mom's convinced Keenan's no good for me.

"All I'm saying is to enjoy your youth while you still can. Trust me when I say that you have the rest of your life to be grown."

I hug my mom tightly and allow her tears to fall onto my bare shoulder. "Priestesses don't get days off," I say, sounding more like Mama than myself. "Besides, I'm enjoying the green eyes. They're quite fierce if I do say so myself."

My mom lifts her head and examines my eyes, searching. "Be careful with your newfound powers, Jayd. Often times the ancestors temporarily gift us with things because we're in grave danger."

The coldest chill ever sweeps over my body, transferring all of my mother's fear into my being. I move my arm; the jade bracelets make a loud clinking sound as they settle on my wrist.

"I can't tell you what to do, Jayd. You came out of me a grown ass woman," my mom says, wiping her face clean. "All I can do is warn you. I may not have my powers the way I used to but I still have a mother's intuition. There are things in this world you're simply not ready to handle, and I think you should allow yourself more time to grow into the powerful woman you're so obviously becoming."

She takes Mama's voodoo doll from my small shrine in the corner of her bedroom and kisses its head. "Please hug Mama for me when you see her. We all miss her presence very much."

"I will," I say, taking the doll. Ironically, those were the last words I spoke to Mama vowing to do the exact opposite of my mother's advice.

I wish I could relax and enjoy the party but nothing is ever that simple for me. I grab my note card with the protection incantation on it, my purse and jacket. "I love you mom. And try not to worry about me. You should know by now that the ancestors have my back." I point to the family veve tattooed on my arm and wink at my mom in an attempt to lighten the mood.

"And you should know by now how the ancestors became ancestors."

Well damn, if that's not a morbid ass thought I don't know what is. My mom's usually the one cheering me up. She kisses me on the forehead and then steps into her bathroom to clean her face.

I check myself in the mirror one more time before heading out the door. "I love you, mom. And don't worry; I've got this." With the spirited words tucked in my right pocket and Mama's doll safely in my possession I think I'll be good.

"You're not as grown as you think you are, Jayd," my mom says from the bathroom door. "Remember that."

My cell buzzes with a call from Chase.

"Hey, I'm on my way now," I say. I kiss my mom on the check and head for the front door.

"Change of plans, Jayd. Can you meet us at the party instead? I'll text you the address."

"Okay, it's closer to my mom's crib anyway." And it'll save me on gas.

"Bet. See you in a few."

I close the door behind me and carefully jog down the stairs only to find Rah waiting at the bottom. This dude is relentless.

"I never you took you for much of a stalker, Rah," I say, hot-tailing it down the driveway toward my mom's ride. We haven't spoken since he attempted to corner me at Mama's house last weekend.

"I thought you might want this back," Rah says, handing me the gold necklace and charm. My neck has felt slightly vacant since that day, but my eleke and veve are all I really need.

"I'm good," I say, refusing his regifting.

"Jayd, would give a nigga a minute, please?" Rah pleads.

I roll my eyes and reluctantly turn around to face my former man, former friend, former everything. "What is it?"

"I wanted us to go the party together tonight." Before I can ask how he knew I was going he answers. "Nigel told me he convinced you to come out for a well-deserved breather."

"Rah, I'm meeting Chase and Nigel at the party. Thanks anyway for the offer."

"Jayd, come on. Can't we just forget about everything and enjoy each other's company for one night? Please?" Rah takes a step closer and reaches out for my hand. I'm afraid that if I take it I'll never let go, and I'm not willing to go backwards. "Come on, Jayd. I already told Trish I was hanging with you tonight and she was cool with it."

Something inside of me snaps at the mention of yet another fool in my life needing permission from some other chick to be with me. "Enough! Rah, I can't take it anymore. You can have all the crazy broads and baby mamas in your life you want to. I'm out. And this time don't send Nigel looking for me because it won't matter. Nothing you say or do can make this right.

"But Jayd, you knew that me and Trish were dating," Rah says, continuing to justify his ill behavior.

"Dated, Rah," I say, correcting his bold lie. "I knew that you dated. Trish will always find a way to sneak back into your world; don't you know that by now? She's a manipulative little trick and that's exactly what she's doing, playing tricks on you."

He looks at me like I've completely lost it but I know my gut's telling me the truth, even if the vision hasn't popped into my head yet. I'm so sick of sneaky rich bitches getting the last word.

"Jayd, just admit that you're jealous," Rah says, flattering himself.

"This is not the time for jokes, Rah," I say, wiping the smug smile from his face. "She's using her brother and Sandy's spawn to get close to you again. And from where I'm standing it's working."

"Jayd, as you've reminded me constantly you're not my girl, so what difference does it make who I see? A brotha can get lonely, too, know what I'm saying?"

"Yeah, I hear you loud and clear," I say, stepping as close to Rah as I can without kissing him. "And let me make myself perfectly clear. It's the heffa or me. You can't have it both ways."

"Jayd, you know I don't do ultimatums, especially not from a girl who claims to only be my friend."

Why am I giving him an ultimatum? Rah's right: He's not my man anymore. Maybe I'm taking all of my frustration out on him, but still he knows this isn't the right thing to do.

"Fine. I'm chucking up the deuces for the last time. Do what you want, Rah. But don't say I told you so when you find out the truth about your dark queen."

"Jayd, don't be that girl who throws a hissy fit because she can't have it her way all the damned time," Rah says to my back. "Lighten up."

"I'm always that girl, Rah," I say, facing him for the last time. "The girl who dudes can call and talk to about their other girls even though they just told me that they loved me a few weeks ago. The girl who always understands why fools do the stupid shit that they do. But no more. I'm done being the ride or die chick who you can tell any and everything to. I don't want to keep any more of your secrets, Rah. Get a diary because I'm through being your paper."

"Don't you think you're being a little dramatic, Jayd? Trish is only Rahima's godmother on paper until I gain custody of Rahima, damn."

"Today it's just for the hearing. Tomorrow you and Trish will be walking down the aisle and she'll be knocked up. You never learn, Rah. You just don't get it, do you?"

"I'm not going out like that, Jayd. I want my daughter to see what a normal family looks like. Me and Kamal didn't have that and never will. But I can do that for my child."

141

"I'm not saying that you can't, Rah. But living a lie isn't going to make anyone happy, least of all Rahima. Don't you think she can tell the difference between real love and temporary lust for show?"

"Call it whatever you like, Jayd. But I'm not going to be a father that plays disappearing acts with his family. It's not happening. And if Sandy wants to marry Trish's brother, I can't do anything about that. But I'll be damned if she takes my daughter with her."

"Lance isn't the problem, Rah. And Sandy will always be Rahima's mother no matter who you end up with. Why does it have to be Trish?"

"Because she's here, Jayd. She's always been here. She never gets mad enough to run away like some people I know. She sticks around when the going gets shitty and I love that about her. And besides, Rahima's known her all of her life."

"Exactly. You never gave me that chance. For whatever reason you think you have to hide important details of your life from me right down to having a baby with my former best friend."

"Here we go again," Rah says, throwing his hands up in the air.

"Am I supposed to forget how you and Sandy met in the first place, when you and I were still a couple?"

"You'll never get tired of having that conversation, will you Jayd? You're going to rub that screw up in my face for the rest of our lives. That's what it would be like to be married to you, Jayd; a conversation on repeat because you never get over shit. People make mistakes, oh mighty one. People trip, fall and get back up but not with you around. You keep stomping a nigga down no matter how many times he tries to make amends."

"That's not true, Rah." Or is it? He sounds a lot like Jeremy, Nigel and Chase for that matter.

"Jayd, you need to look in the mirror and check yourself. Trish doesn't give me any heat for being me and that's what I need up in my house and in my daughter's life. Whoever's going to be around her is going to have to love me as is. Period." Rah tosses the necklace at me, turns around and walks away.

Well I guess he told me. I look at the heavy chain and cry for another broken friendship. I can't blame it all on Esmeralda. Some shit is simply my fault and I have to accept my part in the dissolution of the couple formerly known as Jayd and Rah. We have both officially moved on without each other.

"Maybe you should look more closely at the map next time."
-Emilio
Drama High, volume 10: Culture Clash

~ 14 ~
COLLEGE MATERIAL

When I arrive at the sorority house I notice it boasts the same
letters that I had to endure during my debutante days. Of course Alpha
Gamma Rho is hosting the party. And of course, we're by the hood next
to USC, not at UCLA. I thought we were meeting at a house on Fraternity
Row in Westwood, but apparently Chase had his information mixed up.

I take my spirit notebook out of the glove compartment and read
over my notes for this evening's festivities. I need to say the incantation
three times in the room where everyone I want to protect is present.
Hopefully I can make that happen. It'll be hard to convince Nellie,
Chase, Nigel and Mickey to come together for any reason. And if Rah
decides to make an appearance I'll have to hold my tongue and do the
work. If he tries to step to me again I can cuss him out later.

"Hey beautiful," Chase says, tapping on the passenger's side
window and scaring the hell out of me. Nigel's behind him shaking his
head at how silly our boy can be.

"Chase, what the hell!" I scream. "I know this ain't your territory
but you should know better than to walk up to somebody's car like that.
You can get shot for less."

"What are you going to shoot me with, Jayd? Your journal?" Chase
says, laughing. "Come on, girl. Let's get our college groove on."

I put the notebook up and join my friends for our grand entrance,
even if the tension between them is thicker than the little girl's hair I
braided this afternoon. Mickey and Nellie are in the back of the long

144

line moving toward the front door of the historic house. They're both standing with much attitude. I don't know if their heat is toward each other or just for the boys. Either way they're both emanating quite a bit of it in every direction. I better say this spell quickly before we end up destroying each other, much to Esmeralda's satisfaction.

"What up, my peoples?" Chase says, attempting to break the ice.

Mickey and Nellie nod hello and continue their sulking.

"How you feeling, Nellie?" Nigel asks, concerned about our girl's silence ever since David deserted her.

After her bullying Marcia my sympathy has nearly waned for her mean ass. David's still wrong for whatever went down, but Nellie could push a monk's buttons.

Chase looks bewildered by Nigel's concern for his ex-girlfriend. Chase felt something was wrong with Nellie the other day but she blew him off, as usual.

"How's my daughter?" Nigel asks Mickey, who promptly sucks her teeth.

"I don't know," Mickey says, shifting her weight from one high heel to the other. "Knocked any one up lately?"

"Not funny, Mickey," Nigel says, balling his fists up by his side in frustration. "Not funny at all."

Mickey rolls her hazel contacts at Nigel further fueling the flames. Chase and I look at each other and recognize that we're the only members of our crew with any damned sense right now.

"How is Nickey, Mickey?" I ask, always concerned about my goddaughter's well being. "I've been meaning to spend some time with her."

Nigel hasn't taken his eyes off of Mickey who seems unfazed by his anger.

"She's just fine, at home with her daddy." Mickey looks Nigel dead in the eye and plumps her cleavage to make sure it pops in all the right places. "Mama needed to get out for a change."

"A change?" Nigel yells, ready to pounce. "That's all her mama does is get out and all around." He looks Mickey up and down, disgusted. "And who do you think you are dressing like that to a college party, Miley Cyrus? Go put some clothes on, girl."

Several of the other people in line look at Nigel and await the next verbal blow.

Nellie tries to contain her laughter but a snicker escapes and pisses off her ride home.

"What the hell is so funny, Nellie?" Mickey says.

Nellie quickly checks herself. If she'd just buckle down and get a license she wouldn't need to depend on rides from her friends, and then she could laugh whenever she wanted to.

If Rah's coming he needs to hurry the hell up. I don't know how much longer I can wait to throw these words of protection out. We're not inside yet but I think it'll still work as long as we're all together. The way things are going down we might go our separate ways before we get through the door.

"What up, folk?" Rah says. Speak of the devil. Unfortunately he's brought the witches of Westchester, Trish and Tasha, along for the ride. I guess my rejection was permission to invite his fake wifey after all.

"Nigel," Tasha says, hugging her ex boo. "It's nice to see you."

"Yeah, girl. It's nice to see you, too." He gives Tasha a good once over admiring her tight fitting ensemble: classy yet sexy.

146

I hate to give the heffa props, but Mickey should take notes from Tasha if she wants to be a baller's girl. From the looks of it, Tasha and Nigel might me back on again before the end of the night.

"Jayd," Rah says, forcing me to address him. The mere sound of his voice makes me flustered. I'm not saying he was totally right in his accusations an hour ago but he gave me a lot to think about.

"Rah," I say, attempting to ignore the fact that Trish's arm has moved from by her side to the center of his back, staking her claim for all to see.

Now that everyone's present I can read the card and get this shit over with. The music sounds good from out here but the line is moving at a snail's pace. Most of the people waiting are college students repping their Greek organizations. We stick out like the high school students that we are.

I turn toward the growing crowd and pull out the spell.

"I am the Creator's creation, purely divine. From my enemies I ask that you protect all that I love, all that is mine." I whisper the words three times, ignoring the silence of my friends behind me. I hope that this works soon.

"Jayd, who are you talking to?" Mrs. Esop says, catching me completely off guard. What's she doing at a college party?

"Oh, I was reciting a poem I have to memorize for my English class." Quick lies always work best—I learned that from Rah. "How are you?" I ask, accepting her faux kisses on both of my cheeks.

"I am well," she says. "Nigel, what are you and your friends doing standing outside? You know better than that, son."

"We're just enjoying the view," Nigel says, still gawking at Tasha's figure.

147

"Nigel, be serious," Mrs. Esop says, taking her son's hand. "The next starting quarterback for UCLA does not stand in line, and neither do his friends." She ushers us through the crowd and around the back of the house where the party's really happening. The food looks delicious, and a sistah can always eat.

"Wait a minute." Mrs. Esop does an about face and stops Mickey's advance. "This party is for prospective members and guests only."

"How do you know I ain't going to college?" Mickey says, tugging at her booty shorts.

"Because you say things like 'I ain't' on a regular basis," Mrs. Esop says, unapologetically embarrassing my girl. She's never liked Mickey and now that she's no longer dating her son, whatever tolerance she may have perpetrated is out the door. "And this isn't for simple college students, dear. This party is for prospective black Greeks. Trust me, you're out of your element."

Mickey looks at Nigel who simply smiles and stays silent. His days of defending Mickey are over.

"Mrs. Esop, she's our guest," I say, even if I'm also a guest. "Can you make an exception?"

Mrs. Esop signals for one of the younger sorority sisters to come over and escort us through the tented back yard, again halting Mickey at the gate. "You're not welcome here, Mickey. Go home."

Mickey's eyes fight to stay dry. She must feel as close to shit as one could ever feel, knowing this could've all been hers had she played her cards right. But like so many of us, Mickey has always been her own worst enemy.

148

"Welcome to our house," the polite sistah says, handing us each a pink and red plastic wristband. "We represent the local and college chapters of Alpha Gamma Rho in Southern California."

Mrs. Esop stares Mickey down, unwavering in her decision. I wish I could intervene but this is between the two of them. It'll really be on if Nigel makes good on his promise to sue Mickey for custody of Nickey.

"Who needs this bougie scene anyway," Mickey says, reaching out for Nellie's arm. "Let's bounce."

"But I don't want to go," Nellie says. She looks at me for sympathy but I've got nothing for her. If she thinks I'm giving her a ride back to Compton tonight she's got another think coming. And Nellie knows that Chase is out of the question. He also happens to be Nigel's ride. "Fine," Nellie says, reluctantly following our exiled friend out.

"Damn, that was some cold shit," Chase whispers into my ear.

"That's Mrs. Esop for you," I whisper back. "She's as merciless as they come."

"Will you all be applying to any local schools?" the same young woman asks, gesturing to a table filled with various brochures and other information. I just want to get to the food, damn the formalities.

"I'm thinking of applying to Morehouse or maybe Clark Atlanta," Chase says. Chase is convinced he's going to a historically black college or university to explore his newfound roots. At least his parents can afford to pay the expensive tuition.

"Oh," the girl says, confused. "But those are black colleges."

"I know that," Chase says, a smile spreading across his face. "Where else would I be but with my people?"

"Can't you tell my boy is that pure white chocolate?" Nigel asks, making the girl blush in embarrassment. "It's cool, girl. Don't sweat it."

"Nigel, be good," Mrs. Esop says, pleased that Mickey's a distant distraction in her son's otherwise bright future.

"Oh my goodness, Jayd! Look at you!" a familiar voice screams at the top of her lungs. Me and this girl got into some serious shenanigans back in the day.

"Sam!" I say, returning the love. I've missed her. I was sad when we lost contact after her dad died forcing her mother to move to Orange County. The daily commute to Caldwell Elementary was too much.

"OMG, you're all grown up! And I see you met soror Delilah and our grad advisor, Soror Theresa," Sam says, reintroducing us. "Put your number in my cell right now, girl. We have to catch up."

I pass her my aging cell and we exchange information.

"You know Sam, Jayd?" Mrs. Esop asks, pleased. "Well, isn't this serendipitous. Jayd is one of our star debutantes. She actually won this year's scholarship for partial college tuition and is considering the sisterhood."

"I think my classes and work will keep me busy enough," I say, attempting not to be rude but Mrs. Esop knows where I stand with all of this sorority bull. College is going to be challenging enough without the added social pressure.

"We're not all bad, Jayd. You should check us out," Delilah says, handing me a brochure with their Greek letters on it. "We would love to invite you to our spring social. And if you have any AP credits on your transcripts, you might even be eligible to pledge your first year at UCLA."

"Thank you," I say, being gracious so as not to offend her. Delilah seems nice enough but I know how these sorority girls operate. It could all be a front. The true wench doesn't come out until she gets me on line. "I'll think about it."

"You see, Jayd. I told you that you're college material," Mrs. Esop says, satisfied with her work. "Ladies, we need to check on the girls inside. Enjoy the party." She kisses her son on the cheek and retreats into the lavish home with Sam and Delilah in tow.

"What I miss?" Mickey says, sneaking up behind me.

"I thought you were exiled?" I say, making sure Mrs. Esop doesn't see her. "And where's Nellie?"

"She went to the bathroom to primp, as usual. Look what I found," Mickey says, handing me a red plastic cup with alcohol in it.

"No, thank you," I say, looking around. That's when I notice the man I've been missing all week.

Keenan struts out of the house with some Brazilian looking chick on his arm like he's king of the world. He notices me and smiles big and bright.

"Oh shit," I say, nervously.

"What? Did my former bitch-in-law see me?" Mickey asks like she's hiding from the cops.

"No," I say, sucking in my gut. "Keenan's on his way over."

"Jayd, you made it," Keenan reaches for my right hand and brings it to his lips. "How are you?"

"Just fine, my brotha. Just fine."

"Glad to hear it." He turns toward the chick on his arm and introduces her to my crew. "This beautiful woman is Sadie, the president of the SC chapter of Alpha Gamma Rho."

"It's nice to meet you both," Sadie says, lying through her way too white grill. I can tell she's disgusted by our young presence.

151

"Let me get you something to drink, Jayd," Keenan asks, ever the polite host. "Mickey, you good?"

"Yeah, I'm cool." Mickey takes a large swig from her cup and looks around the party. I can tell she's ready to set it off.

"So, you're the fresh meat of the week," Keenan's arm candy says, displaying her true colors.

I have no problem setting a college heffa straight if need be, but Mickey takes the lead on this one.

"Jayd's not fresh meat but I can pound you like ground beef if you like."

Sadie looks at us like the hoodrats we seemingly are right now. The chick knows Mickey's not playing.

Alcohol always brings out the worst in Mickey and she's fiery enough as is. Maybe Mickey should go on a twelve-step program like Jeremy was forced into as a part of his probation.

"Excuse me. I see someone I need to greet," Sadie says, walking over to Nigel, Rah and their dates. She hugs Nigel who looks like he knows Sadie very well.

"I'm tired of that nigga," Mickey says, throwing her cup down on the ground. He can kiss my ass."

I roll my eyes at Mickey. "I think he already did."

Mickey glares at me like I'm lying. She knows she messed up and has no one to blame but herself. "I'm going to find me something else to drink."

Mickey walks toward the back of the sprawling yard where I spot Nellie. She checks her cell and I swear her face has turned three shades lighter. I wish she'd look up at me so that I can read her thoughts. I'd put all my money on those texts being from David.

"What are you doing here?" KJ asks with some college broad on his arm, which is no surprise. If I were KJ I'd watch my step. Misty's powers are growing and I'm assuming her jealous temper hasn't cooled off a bit since we were friends. Speak of the devil, out walks Misty. Why the hell is everyone from the South Central side of South Bay High present at this party?

"I was invited, do you mind?" I say, taking a step closer to Keenan.

"It's just virgin punch," Keenan says, handing me the cup. "I didn't take you for a drinker."

"I'm not, thank you," I say, taking a sip. Maybe I've been too hard on Keenan. Compared to my track record, Keenan's a winner.

"Everything about Jayd is virgin, my nigga," KJ says, laughing at his crass joke.

Before Keenan can kick his ass my nemesis approaches her ex with enough hate to handle him for us all.

"KJ," Misty says, cutting her blue eyes at him and placing her hands on her full hips.

KJ smiles at Misty as she takes his other arm without checking for the broad he's already attached to. There must be something going on that I don't know about, and I'm just fine being ignorant to Misty's mysteries—she's always full of surprises.

"Jayd, what a surprise," Misty says, kissing her ex-man on the cheek. "They're just letting anyone into supposedly exclusive parties these days, aren't they?"

"I'm sorry," Keenan says, invading Misty's space. "And you're a guest of whom?"

Misty looks at KJ but he's not falling for her games. He detaches himself from her and ignores her need for an escort. She dumped him for Emilio and eventhough I know Misty's at the whim of Esmeralda, KJ doesn't. All he feels is betrayed and—like Nigel—his days of including his ex in his new life are over.

"I was invited, trust that," Misty says. She looks at me with pure hatred. I can't help it that she showed up to a college party without the proper credentials.

The pretty chick Keenan strutted outside with walks over and lays down the law.

"KJ, is she on your guest list?" she asks, giving Misty the same look Mrs. Esop gave Mickey. KJ's a prospective basketball recruit giving him free rein here much like he has at South Bay.

"Nope," KJ says, hugging up on his new broad. "But my boys should be arriving soon."

Sadie turns to Misty who doesn't look the least bit intimidated. "If you're not with an invited guest you have to leave."

I wasn't feeling this chick at first but now she's my best friend.

"Keenan, we need to call the caterers and order more food. We're way over capacity."

"I'm on it." Keenan begins to walk inside but not before handling Misty. "And I do hope you get home safely," Keenan says, pointing toward the back gate.

"Whatever," Misty says, rolling her eyes at KJ who ignores her. Without much of a protest Misty walks toward the back entrance. Before she makes a clean exit she doubles back and addresses me. "Is that a car alarm I hear?"

Several people look out of the gate to check for their cars but the sound continues. I pull out my keys and push the alarm button. The noise stops immediately.

"My mom's car!" I say, running toward the shattered glass on the curb. The passenger's window is busted, the tires are flattened, the speakers have been ripped out of the doors and my leather jacket is gone. There was nothing else in the car worth taking; I put my iPod and accessories in my purse pocket.

"Damn, Jayd," Mickey says, sipping on something else she has no business drinking. "I'm sorry but you know it's one of the consequences of parking in the hood, no matter how much they tried to fix up this side of LA."

Don't I know it? This car's been broken into several times over the past few years, usually right in the parking garage at my mom's apartment building. But with all of the flyy cars lined up and down this street the thieves chose mine. This is definitely personal and there's only one person who would be interested in seeing me cry: Misty by way of Esmeralda.

"Why you got to go and say some insensitive shit like that?" Nigel says to Mickey. He and Chase followed me out front with a small crowd behind them.

"Watch how you talk to me, boy," Mickey says, belligerently tipping her red cup at him.

"I got your boy," Nigel says, ready to check Mickey, damn the consequences.

All of my friends and a few nosey onlookers stare on as I try to make sense of what's happening. I think I did something wrong when writing my incantation because it has failed miserably.

"Is everything okay?" Keenan asks, coming out with his cell to his ear.

I break down, completely sobbing in Keenan's arms.

"Jayd, it's going to be okay," Keenan says, hanging up his call and wrapping his strong arms around me. I'm getting his Sean John long sleeved shirt wet, but Keenan pulls me in closer, unconcerned about his attire.

My friends try to keep each other from getting dragged too far into Mickey and Nigel's raging argument. Mrs. Esop's going to flip when she gets wind of this, which should be any moment.

"When is it, Keenan, because I can't take much more?" I don't know what to do about Misty, Mama or anyone else close to me, and I failed at my first solo task as a priestess without my grandmother here to help. "I hate this shit."

He strokes my hair, listening to every word. "Come on, Jayd. Let's get you out of here. I'll call my automobile club to tow your car wherever you want it to go."

"But what about the party?" I ask, looking around as Mickey gets more hoodrat by the minute. This isn't a good look for Nigel whose mom charges out of the front door as we speak.

"I think it's taking a turn for the worst," Keenan says as Mrs. Esop removes her hostess apron and passes it to his earlier escort. "Come on. My truck's parked up the block. Besides, we haven't had a chance to talk much lately."

I look around at the chaos continuing to unfold and choose to separate myself from my broken friends. It's not my fault they don't know how to act in public, but I definitely feel partially responsible for not being able to stop the shit before it hit the sorority house.

"Can you have my car towed to my mom's?" I ask, following Keenan.

"Whatever you need, Jayd," Keenan says, holding my hand. "I got you."

"I'm deflowered and I gave it up to the wrong person."
-Nellie
Drama High, volume 13: The Meltdown

~15~
GROWN ASS

"Welcome to my home," Keenan says, flipping the light switch on to reveal the neat bachelor pad.

"Wow," I say, in awe of his space. It's an upstairs single apartment. The long entrance opens up to walls filled with DVDs, CDs, records and magazines with a tall column of books in each corner.

"If a thief came in here he'd be very disappointed." Keenan smiles and opens the deep brown curtains revealing a perfect view of Westwood and UCLA.

"Don't be so sure," I say, placing my purse down on his desk. "That's what I used to say about my mom's ride."

"I'm sorry about everything that happened tonight, Jayd," Keenan says, dimming the lights. "At least the car's safe and sound at your mom's apartment." Keenan passes me a music catalogue and the remote to his iPod dock next to the small couch at the foot of his bed.

"There's no such thing as safe for me." I toss the music collection onto the couch and blindly press play.

"Fela. Good choice," he says, joining me by the window.

"It's just not right." I look out into the darkness and feel lost yet I know I'm on the right path. I guess that's how Mama felt in her last dream. She was clearly out of character but swears she was in control.

"It certainly feels right to me," Keenan says.

I stare back at Keenan's reflection in the glass, my green eyes searching for his true intentions. Does this brotha know the only thing keeping me from invading his mind is my self-control?

"No offense, but when you walked in with that chick tonight I was a little taken aback."

"Who, Sadie?" Keenan turns me around by the waist. "She's just a friend and a partner in good deeds, if you will."

"She's a stunningly voluptuous Brazilian college broad who you see on a regular basis. I'm not exotic and never will be."

"Jayd, girls like that are a dime a dozen around here. To find a passionate, conscious, intelligent, mysterious, and damn fine sistah like you is rare, green contacts and all," Keenan says, making me blush.

"Keenan, there's a lot going on in my world that you don't know about."

"Then enlighten me, Jayd. Please."

"I don't know if you'd still feel me the same way if I told you everything." Keenan has been a good friend, even coming to Pam's homegoing ceremony when he didn't know her. He should be able to handle all the crazy that comes with being friends with a priestess.

My confession is almost ready to pour out but Keenan cuts it short by kissing me. I take in every movement of his full lips. He gently bites my bottom lip and then kisses my throat.

"Yes, Jayd. I feel you." Keenan nibbles at the base of my neck and continues moving south.

"You know what I mean," I say, bringing his head back up to my lips. I take control, this time kissing him passionately in return.

We fall onto the couch where I'm still in control. I've never felt a surge of energy like this toward anyone before. My hips move like my ancestors' to the drums beating in the background. The saxophone cries out and increases the song's tempo. Keenan lifts me up and places me on my back in one swift move. Football sure does his body good.

"Keenan," I moan, breaking away only to again get caught up in his gaze.

I stare into his brown eyes and see my own in the reflection. I don't recognize the woman staring back at me. What am I doing? I know I should be focused on my failed work and not this moment no matter how good it feels. Unfortunately, I don't belong to myself right now, not until Mama's completely healthy and my eyes are back to brown.

"Are you on birth control?" Keenan says, directing my movements. He's ready to prove KJ wrong and I want to let him, but I can't stop thinking about all of my issues.

"I'm sorry, Keenan," I say, easing from up under him. "It's just not the right time for this."

"I don't understand," Keenan says, pecking my cheek. "I thought this was going so well." He moves to my ear nearly incapacitating me.

"Keenan, I've got too much on my mind. I should probably go," I say, pushing him off of me. I try to get up but Keenan pulls me down onto his lap and holds me.

"No pressure, Jayd. Tomorrow I'll take you anywhere you want to go, but it's too late to go anywhere tonight."

"Keenan, thank you." I place my head on his shoulder and relax. I'm grateful that he's so understanding. The time will come for me to make love and when it does I want to be in my right mind.

"So, what's the main thing on your mind, Jayd?" Keenan asks, settling down. "And I know it's not your car or your friends."

I know I can't divulge all of my family goods but I can tell him the gist of it. "My grandmother's neighbor, Esmeralda has the upper hand in a long-standing feud between her family and mine. Until I figure out how to get control of the situation I can't let myself relax, no matter how much I may want to."

"Well then, I say we pull an all night brainstorming session until we figure this shit out, because this Esmeralda lady is messing up my flow and we can't have that."

"Oh really?" I say, playfully pinching him in the side.

"Ouch, girl!" he says, grabbing my hands. "You know what I mean."

"Yes, I do." I kiss Keenan and he returns the affection. We'd better stop before we find ourselves too far gone again.

"Okay, I'm all ears," Keenan says, backing up. Even if he can't help with the spiritual side, he may see something that I can't and I need all the help I can get.

Keenan listened to me talk all about mi vida loca and didn't try anything else for the rest of the night. He actually gave me some very insightful suggestions on how to handle all the drama I seem to find myself in the middle of, including shaking my crew for good. We fell asleep on that impossible note. I've considered a total rebirth more than once since starting my senior year. So far, I like the life that Keenan's introducing me to, which happens to be very similar to the same reality Mrs. Esop wants me to be a part of.

I'm surprised that he left me in his apartment all alone. If Mickey or Nellie were left in a dude's home without supervision they'd take it as an opportunity to snoop and call each other for blow-by-blow details of what they think they found. I see it two ways: I wouldn't want anyone invading my privacy like that, and you never know where the cameras could be hidden. Call me paranoid, but I don't put anyone above spying. Trust, I had to resist the urge to snoop but I figure Keenan wouldn't leave me alone in his space if he had something to hide.

"I hope you like coffee and donuts," Keenan says, forcing me up. He slept on the couch allowing me to completely take over his bed. Keenan's so sweet to let me sleep in while he ventured blocks away to get us the most famous and affordable pastries in Westwood.

"Sounds perfect," I say, reaching for a paper cup and glazed donut. "And thanks for the sleep over. I haven't slept that soundly in months."

"Glad to be of service." Keenan claims a sugar twist and coffee and joins me on the bed. "I hope the conversation was helpful, too."

"Oh, it was," I say, taking a big bite of my breakfast. "And if nothing else you brought clarity on my friends' situations."

"I hope Nigel's as receptive when we meet later on at the football meeting. The coach and older players have to sit down with all of the new recruits and check for their futures."

"Nigel's future's on lock; no worries there," except for his love of all things shiny no matter where they come from, but Keenan doesn't need to know about the unsolicited gifts Nigel's accepting from other interested schools. I'm sure he had the same thing happen to him when he was on the draft list.

"Were you not at the same party I was last night where his hoodrat of a baby mama caused a scene, with his mother in the house no less?"

"She's not a hoodrat," I say, defending my friend even if he's telling the truth. "Her name's Mickey and she's actually very sweet when she wants to be."

"Yeah, okay," Keenan says, digging into a cake donut, one of my favorites. "And then there's his best friend, Rah."

"What about Rah?" I ask, taking a piece of his donut. "They're like brothers and he definitely gets Mrs. Esop's seal of approval."

"He's a thug and Nigel would be wise to shake him before it ruins his career. I had to let go of my friends from the old neighborhood for the same reason. Every smart athlete has a talk with himself about what he wants to achieve and the sacrifices needed to get him there."

"What's that supposed to mean?" I ask, defensively. I don't like the sound of this meeting.

"It means, like I told you last night, that some things have to go in order for you to grow—friends included. Do you want the last donut or can we split it?" Keenan asks, making light of the fact that my entire world has shifted right before my eyes.

"You can take your donut and your opinion about my friends and stick them wherever you want," I say, kicking the covers back and getting out of the bed.

"Jayd, don't be like that," he says, taking me by the hand. "I just think you should choose the company you keep very carefully. Listen, why don't you come to a study session with me and my friends this week. Let me show how grown people hang."

I want to be mad at Keenan, but every time he pulls me into him all of my doubts disappear.

"This is exactly what I was talking about, Jayd. That boy's got more mojo than you're ready to deal with, girl. We'll talk about where you are and what y'all were doing last night later, with your grown ass," my mom says sternly into my thoughts. Five minutes later and I would've been out of here. But no, she had to chime in at just the wrong time. I'll never be

able to loose my virginity with my two moms up in my head whenever they please. *"Meet me at Dr. Whitmore's in an hour."*

"But mom, your car is incapacitated again," I think without disclosing all of the details. *"And I hate taking the bus, especially on the weekends."*

My mom's mental pause speaks volumes.

"I better get home," I say, standing. I need to change out of the football shorts and t-shirt he gave me to sleep in and back into my own clothes. "Do you mind dropping me off at my mom's?"

"Of course not. But you didn't answer me about coming to campus this week. You know I love showing you off."

I reclaim last night's outfit draped across the arm of the couch and head for the bathroom. "Okay, it's a study date."

I think about all of the shit that's gone down lately. Maybe Keenan's right about me changing the crowd I roll with. I know Misty had something to with my car getting broken into. I'm also over Mickey and Nellie giving me attitude whenever the mood suits them. Hell, if it weren't for Mickey's trifling ways Mama and I would've never been in that legal mess with Mrs. Esop. But contrary to Mickey's and Mama's thoughts about Nigel's mom, Mrs. Esop kept her part of the bargain and I have to keep mine. What kind of person would I be without my word?

~16~
DADDY'S BABY, MAMA'S MAYBE

Even though I know last night's break in was more than bad luck it was yet another reminder that I need to buy my own ride. Shakir's offer to sponsor my hair business out of the back of Simply Wholesome sounds better every day. A little independence—and more money—is just what the doctor ordered.

My mom's mailbox is barely closed due to all of the bills stuffed inside. I rarely check it since what little mail I do have goes to Mama's address but this is ridiculous. As soon as I turn the small lock a package falls to the ground along with several envelopes and advertisements.

"University of California, Los Angeles," I read aloud. The blue letters look foreign to me. I didn't request any information from this school. How did the admissions office get my mom's address anyway?

There's so much to do before I turn in my applications online. I still have to take the SAT, work on my essays, résumé and letters of recommendation not to mention fill out the financial aid information for both of my parents. The most difficult of all my tasks will be deciding which schools to apply to. Daddy's church program only pays for the first ten and I'm not planning on going past that number. Free always sounds good to me.

"Can you believe this shit?" Mickey says, pulling into the driveway and waving a large manila envelope out of her window. Apparently Mickey's dealing with a special delivery of her own.

"What are you doing on this side of town?" I ask, relocking the box. Mickey rarely travels to the Westside.

"I came to kick Nigel's ass and I need back up," Mickey says, reaching across the passenger's side and unlocking the door. Her classic car doesn't have the modern conveniences Chase had installed into his equally old ride.

"Mickey, I'm not getting involved in whatever ongoing beef you've got with my boy." I step off of the porch and walk past Mickey's car toward my mom's apartment.

"Are you wearing the same thing you had on last night?" Mickey asks. Even in the midst of her blind rage she's still fashion conscious much like her BFF, Nellie.

"Yes, and I'm going upstairs to change before I handle some business of my own."

"Jayd, you have to come with me," Mickey says, slowly following me. "Nigel's demanding that I take Nickey in for a paternity test. Is this nigga serious?"

"Well, you did challenge him," I say. "And with Mrs. Esop in his corner Nigel might have a valid case." If Mama and I didn't have that je no sais quoi with Chase's mom, Mrs. Esop might be a partner in Netta's Never Nappy Beauty Shop as we speak.

"Whose side are you on, Jayd?"

"Nickey's," I say, matter-of-factly. In case she doesn't know I need to remind her again that I'm here for the good her daughter, damn the rest.

"I can't stand up to them alone," Mickey says, sounding vulnerable. "I can't let them take my daughter, Jayd. Please come with me. And I'm sorry about what happened to your mom's car last night. I'll take you anywhere you want to go after we leave Nigel's house."

A ride to hell incarnate, or ride the bus from Inglewood to Compton on a hot Saturday afternoon: tough choice but one will probably take much longer than the other. Besides, maybe I can talk some sense into both of them before it's too late. "Give me five minutes."

When we pull up to the mini mansion in Lafayette Square I notice Chase's Nova parked in the driveway. Mrs. Esop's in her rose garden, her usual spot on a sunny day. She looks up over her sunglasses as we walk up the long driveway; her expression is anything but welcoming.

"Jayd, why on Earth would you bring that girl to our home?" Mrs. Esop asks, like I drove here. "You know she's not welcomed on my property."

"Good morning, Mrs. Esop," I say, attempting to be cordial.

"Good morning my ass," Mickey says, ending the niceties. "Where's your son? We need to talk."

"He's right where he should be," Mrs. Esop says looking at her pristine flora. "Far away from you."

"I thought I smelled a hoodrat," Nigel says, appearing in the front doorway. Chase nods what up at me and disappears into the background. "I see you got the package. Gotta love FedEx."

"You can go straight to hell, Nigel!" Mickey screams. "You're not taking my baby away from me!" She attempts to open the screen door but it's locked.

Nigel laughs at Mickey's reaction. He's getting way too much pleasure out of seeing his ex loose it this early in the morning. This is so

167

unlike him. My crew doesn't know it but Esmeralda's spell is working too well and their ever-present drama's making it easy for her to completely take over our lives.

"Did your friend here tell you that G knew about Mickey and Tre's affair all along?" Nigel asks, dropping knowledge. "He didn't mind killing his own friend, Jayd. That's who Mickey chose to shack up with; a punk ass gangsta who killed his own boy, the same boy who saved my life."

"Mickey, is this true?" I ask, appalled at the disclosure. "Please tell me Nigel's got it wrong."

Mickey looks shell-shocked not knowing what to say, but what can she say? Nothing can make that shit sound good if it's the truth.

Mrs. Esop looks at Mickey break down and shakes her head at the pitiful sight.

"Hell yeah it's true," Nigel says. "She let everybody know it at the party last night. It was her final confession before she threw up everywhere, stupid drunk."

"Nigel, manners," Mrs. Esop says, always the etiquette police.

"How you gone try to come up in my life and take my baby, fool?" Mickey says, snapping back into full angry-black-woman mode. "My baby, Nigel! Not yours in any way, shape or form."

"You should've thought of that before you tried to convince my son otherwise," Mrs. Esop says from the sidelines.

Mickey's neck snaps hard in her direction but she's not crazy enough to respond to Mrs. Esop. She doesn't need pruning shears to chop Mickey down to size and Mickey knows it.

"Exactly my point, mom," Nigel says, satisfied.

168

"You need to kick rocks, you little bitch," Mickey says. "I got this; me and my man." It's one thing when a female calls another female a bitch. Hell, it's even more tolerable when a dude calls a female a bitch. But when it happens in the reverse, it's a whole other beast.

"What did you say to me, trick?" Nigel says, opening the screen door. I've been waiting for his other shoe to drop and here it is, as funky as ever. I warned Mickey about pushing Nigel too far. Mostly he takes after his father's cool side but Nigel can be a real jerk when he wants to be.

"You heard me, you little bitch. My man was right about you. That's his pet name for you, you know: my little puppy dog, hound dog ass bitch."

Mrs. Esop rises from her garden and removes her sun hat, ready to whip ass if need be: Compton never left the woman no matter what her new zip code may be.

"Mickey, I think we should go," I say, trying to save Mickey's neck and Nigel's sanity. She has no idea how close to the edge he is right now.

"Mickey, you need to calm down," Chase says, stepping outside in an attempt to further warn Mickey, but she's really feeling herself this morning.

"What I need to do is kick your punk ass so hard that you'll never be able to have your own babies. That'll teach you to mess with somebody else's kid."

"You need to talk some sense into your girl, Jayd. Now." Something in Nigel's tone puts everything into perspective and I don't like what I see.

Thanks to Maman's sight immediate future events play out like movie scenes in my head: Mickey kicks Nigel, Nigel slaps Mickey hard to the ground, and then the police are called. Nigel goes to jail and looses any chance he has of getting into UCLA or any other school, Mickey looses custody of her daughter for being an unfit parent, and Esmeralda wins round two.

"Mickey, you've got to chill out, for real," I say, pulling Mickey's arm toward the car but she's not budging.

"What's Nigel going to do, Jayd?" Mickey says, snatching her arm away from me. "He can't do a damned thing to me or my baby, punk ass fool. He needs to come off of his high horse and apologize for leaving me and my baby at Rah's house without him. Rah wanted to act like my daddy all the time, telling me what time to put Nickey to bed and what to feed her, blah blah blah. No wonder Sandy left his ass," Mickey says. Did I just hear her side with Sandy when just a few months ago she was putting Sandy's stuff out on the curb at Rah's house? What the hell?

"Mickey, do you hear yourself talking?" I ask, trying to snap her out of it. "You sound like you're losing it again. Have you been taking your meds?"

"Whatever, Jayd," Mickey says, evading my question about Dr. Whitmore's post-natal prescription. Esmeralda's diabolical vitamins jacked her up and I had to undo that mess, too. "I'm finally seeing Nigel for the chump that he is. I'm filing for child support, since you want to be the baby daddy so bad. That'll show you that I'm not to be messed with."

"Go right ahead and do that, little girl," Mrs. Esop says, joining her son on the porch steps. "It'll just make our case that much stronger against you, you little gold digging hussy."

I step in front of Mickey and face her, preventing her from taking another step forward. She's going to look me in the eye and chill out whether she likes it or not.

"I'm not afraid of you, Mrs. Esop," Mickey shouts over my shoulder. "You think you run the world but you don't run shit. Hell, you couldn't even keep your son from leaving your house with all of that damn money y'all are sitting on. If you had just let us move in when I said so wouldn't be in this damn mess right now."

"Really, Mickey?" Chase says, tired of the bull. "That's what got you into this mess?"

"Yes, white boy. It really is."

"No, Mickey. Your lying and cheating is what got us all into this mess on so many levels. Wake up and take responsibility for once in your life," I say, snapping my fingers in her face.

"You're crazy, Jayd," Mickey says, slapping my hand away. "I should've known you'd take his side, you little traitor."

"I'd rather be crazy and happy than sane and sad any day," I say after Mickey who's charging toward her car. Mickey can have that shit if she wants it. I personally don't see the point in creating more friction than need be. Life's already difficult enough as it is.

"Sorry I'm late," I say, rushing inside Dr. Whitmore's office. I drop my bag on the futon and give my grandmother a hug.

"That Chase is a sweet boy to drop you off," Netta says as Chase's car loudly pulls away from the curb. "Your mama told us what happened with her car."

"Yeah, he's a good friend, unlike Mickey who left me at Nigel's house after she begged me to go with her. That's the last time I do Mickey any favors."

171

"What happened now?" Mama asks as she beats cornbread batter in a large, red clay bowl. I hope that's for us and not just the ancestors. I've missed Mama's cooking.

"She went off on Nigel and Mrs. Esop who of course set her straight, further enraging her perpetually hot head," I say, reliving the memory. "If anyone can take Mickey's daughter from her it's Mrs. Esop, forget biology."

"Leave it to Teresa to start some shit," Netta says, snapping green beans. "She always wants to be somebody's mama."

"This time it wasn't her fault," I say, walking over to the small washbowl and cleaning my hands and face like I do when I walk into Netta's shop. "I can't believe I'm defending her, but Mickey was way out of pocket today. Way, way out of line."

"Speaking in being out of line, I heard you spent the night with that Keenan person," Netta says, snapping the peas harder than necessary. "What's that all about?"

"Yes, do tell," Mama says, setting the bowl down. "Your mama has voiced her concerns over this friend of yours more than once, which makes me very concerned."

"My mom is overreacting." Where is she anyway? She told me to meet her here and then leaves me to the firing squad alone after dropping all of my business.

"She went to the church with your grandfather," Mama says, dropping a bomb of her own. "She and Karl wanted to get his blessing and decide on a final date for the ceremony. She wanted you to go with her but you were late."

"Mickey," I whisper under my breath. I want to be there for my mom and Karl but life keeps getting in the way.

"That girl didn't put a gun to your head, Jayd," Netta says, unsympathetically. "You have to learn when to say no and let it be."

"Absolutely, especially to these little friends of yours, including that boy." Mama takes a cast iron skillet from the pot rack hanging from the ceiling in the small kitchen adjacent to the main room and wipes it clean with her apron.

"You keeping your legs closed, little girl?" Netta asks, taking down a stainless steel pot for the beans.

"Yes, ma'am," I say. They don't need to know that I'm thinking about doing the opposite.

"Well, when you do decide to take that extra step into womanhood do it with all of your power in place," Mama says, pouring the gold batter into the buttered skillet. "And make sure that you don't give your love to anybody unless you're sure he's ready to receive it." Mama's so wise and her advice is right on time.

"The grill's warming up," Dr. Whitmore says, stepping inside from the back. "Afternoon, Jayd."

"Good afternoon, Dr. Whitmore," I say, noticing him notice Mama. They exchange a knowing look and he heads back outside.

"Mama, what's that all about?" I ask. Mama blushes and continues with today's lesson.

"Your imagination's running wild, child," Netta says, taking some of the heat from her friend but I know what I saw.

"Like all of the women in our lineage, you've got all the right working parts. I am well aware that you're a beautiful young woman and will always attract a lot of attention."

"Just like your grandmother and mama," Netta says, winking at her best friend for life.

Mama rolls her eyes at Netta. "I know you can go out there and do whatever the hell you want to. My concern is who you do it with, and also that you come out of it as healthy as you were when you went in. I'd be lying if I said I felt comfortable with this Keenan boy all of a sudden being your new best friend when you're still getting over Rah and Jeremy."

"When you say it like that I feel like a slut and I haven't even done anything yet," I say, suddenly feeling bad. It has been a busy few months.

"No one's saying all of that," Mama says, placing the skillet in the oven. "All I'm saying is to slow down and think about the consequences of your actions. It's like playing chess: Plan three steps ahead and you'll always win the game."

"It's a merciless game, that's for sure." I sigh, tired of the repeated heartbreaks.

"Baby, love has no mercy on our hearts. Not at all," Mama says, touching the crossed heart charm hanging at the end of my eleke. "Love is merciless yet it depends on our ability to forgive for it's very survival. Ain't that some irony for your ass? When you go in you have to go all the way in, damn the consequences. At times love will hurt so bad you'll think you're going to die. And that's also how good it feels on the other side."

"That's the truth, Jayd. And what your grandmother's not saying is that sex is wonderful when it's with the right person," Netta says, filling the pot with water and placing it on the stove. Dinner's going to be delicious. Too bad we still have a few hours before that happens.

"One day we'll talk about men and things, but not right now," Mama says, glaring at Netta who shrugs her shoulders. One day I'll have to have some alone time with my godmother to get the real talk.

"Why not?" I want to hear about the men in Mama's life, including Dr. Whitmore. Anyone with eyes can see that they have a special chemistry.

"Because there are still some things you're too young to understand and I'm not comfortable talking in detail about with anyone your age," Mama says. "Just know this: Life is untidy, Jayd. What you think is wrong can suddenly become the most appealing decision you've ever encountered. And once your innocence is lost it's gone forever, no matter how it happens, and power comes as a byproduct of this transformation. Good or bad, womanhood is power."

"Just look at your friend Mickey," Netta says, taking the spirit book off of the shelf, ready to get into our real work for the afternoon. "That girl wasn't ready for her crown, but she has to wear it, no matter how heavy it is."

"That's why I can't understand how I'm supposed to know when it's the right time and the right person." I thought Rah would be my first, then I met Jeremy. That hasn't worked out very well, and I'm attracted to Keenan but something tells me that he's not the one, either.

"When it's right you'll know," Netta says, flipping through the pages of the ancient book. She's the only non-Williams woman allowed to touch our family manuscript. "The stars will align, the birds will sing and there will be no fear in your heart." Netta laughs at her over-dramatized rendition of losing one's virginity, but I know it's supposed to be more like that than what Nellie and Mickey experienced.

"Your silly godmother is right about one thing, Jayd: In relationships, it is the fear that hurts, not the love. Love never hurts, except when people are afraid to give or receive it."

Well if that's the case, that rules out both Rah and Jeremy.

"It's up to you to listen to your spirit when choosing," Netta says, handing the book over to Mama.

"I've always chosen the wrong men. Well, except maybe once or twice," Mama says, recalling a memory I wish I could snatch up. "But other than that I seem to have made a habit of choosing the same stupid ass man time and time again, just in a different body until I met your grandfather, of course," Mama says, winking at me. I know Mama and Daddy have had their fair share of indiscretions but they always seem to find their way back to each other.

"It is true, the man who makes love to you until you scream out in both pain and pleasure is the one who can lock you down and make you stupid in love if you let him," Mama says, reading my thoughts. "But the choice is still yours if you choose to exercise it. No need in trying to figure the shit out. It is what it is. The only thing I can do is pray for the spirit of discernment to sit with you, take over what you think you know and show you the right way. As soon as spirit says run, run. As soon as spirit says be quiet, shut up. As soon as spirit says stay, sit your ornery ass down somewhere and be still. Your heart was not meant to be worn on a sleeve, Jayd. Protect it at all cost."

Talk about hitting two birds with one stone. Mama's right on all fronts, as usual.

"Sometimes it's better to leave love out of the equation until you're strong enough to handle it without getting handled by it," Netta says.

"Okay, ladies. Enough chatter. We have several orders to fill for our clients before we can enjoy dinner. Jayd, please gather the strawberries and baking soda for the teeth whitening paste. Ms. Newson's about to have a fit if we don't fill her monthly order."

I do as I'm told and consider all that they've given me to think about. I wish Jeremy and I could work our issues out because as of now, he's the only one in my heart and on my mind if I'm honest with myself. Maybe my confession about Cameron's evil doings on Friday wasn't such a bad thing after all. The sooner her conniving ass is checked once and for all, the better. Jeremy still has a lot to learn about courage under fire but when it's all said and done, I choose him. Jeremy and I can discuss our future after tonight's study session, Cameron be damned.

"I don't much believe in things I can't see."
-Jeremy
Drama High, volume two: Second Chance

~ 17 ~
CURIOUS WHITE BOY

Mama insisted that I come back to the spirit room before heading to Redondo Beach for the evening. Mrs. Bennett assigned a test for this Wednesday and everyone's in a panic, even her favorite students. If it weren't for Marcia texting me earlier about the Facebook announcement for the study group I would've never known. Marcia may turn out to be a good new friend after all.

"What up, niecey?" Bryan asks, scaring me half to death.

"Nothing much. Just feeding the shrines before I head to the bus stop," I say, slightly bitter that I'm back on public transportation. But if all goes well this evening I'll be able to count on Jeremy for a ride home. "What's up with you?" I invite him in.

"Me and the wifey have plans before I go to work at the radio station tonight," Bryan says, stepping inside of the small house to check his reflection. "A brotha looks irresistible, doesn't he?"

"He's aight," I say, playing with my favorite uncle. He does look nice in his khaki pants and crisp, white shirt. His braids are also quite flyy, courtesy of his favorite niece.

"Yeah, the wifey's going to be impressed."

The sound of Esmeralda's back door slamming shut causes us both to look out of the window into her backyard where I can see Misty and Emilio sweeping the back porch. Esmeralda's got skills when it comes to mind control, no doubt.

"Are you okay, Jayd?" he asks, pointing at my luminescent sight.

"I'm fine," I lie. I check my reflection in the wall mirror and admire the green glow. "They've been doing that a lot lately."

Misty stops what she's doing and stares across the yard. Our eyes lock; hers intensely blue, and my jade ones shining strong.

Bryan looks across the way and notices the energy exchange; so does Emilio who is now an involuntary participant in our energy triangle.

"Jayd, what the hell is going on?" Bryan asks, trying to shake me free but I don't want to let go. Misty's no match for Maman.

"Don't worry, unc. I've got this." I relax into the powers as the cool feeling completely takes over, manipulating Misty's assumed powers. I easily maneuver through her thoughts with her none the wiser to what she's giving up, which isn't much. Whatever Esmeralda's using to keep Misty on lock is also keeping my nemesis in the dark.

Remembering my walk through Emilio's sight I lock onto his hazel eyes and allow Misty to continue her ineffective probing on me. He's the perfect mule because he has no powers of his own: Emilio's powers are in his drawings. I can see him drawing veves for Esmeralda's ceremonies. Both his grandmother and godfather are present to provide the cornmeal and Florida water needed to create the images on the ground. Once his work is done Misty steps into the center of the picture and lends her power to a voodoo doll given to her by her godmother.

"Esmeralda can't empower the dolls herself," I say aloud. I can feel Bryan look at me and shake his head. He knows better than to mess with me and Mama when we get down like this.

At Esmeralda's verbal command her man pet comes outside and breaks our link without knowing what occurred. I can only imagine what would've happened to Mr. Gatlin if Esmeralda kept her claws in him much longer. He's not my favorite neighbor but I still don't wish any ill will on him.

"Thank you," I say to the ancestor shrines. Now I see why Mama had me come back here when she did. Something good always happens after we make a sacrifice.

"I don't even want to know what that was all about," Bryan says, helping me lock up.

"It was about revenge," I say, quickly glancing at Misty who smiles in return. She has no idea what she's getting into but she and her evil ile are about to find out.

"Do you remember the time we were walking down the street and Misty gave you a compliment?" Bryan asks, walking me toward the back gate. Lexi comes out of the bushes and tags along. I know she misses her master terribly; anyone can tell that she's miserable without Mama.

"I think I do. Why do you ask?"

"Because I think she wants to be just like you," Bryan says, making me question the entire episode I just had with my frenemy. "If that's the case, then you have the upper hand in whatever it is y'all got going on."

"I don't understand what you mean."

"Of course you do," Bryan says, spitting sunflower seed shells onto the sidewalk, officially undermining his fresh appearance. "The one thing Misty wants more than anything that I can think of is to be just like you."

"Where'd you get that idea from?"

"It's obvious, Jayd. From the first time y'all met the girl's been trying to rock how you roll. Trust your elder when he speaks," Bryan

180

says, pinching my cheek like I'm five years old. "To beat Misty at her own game all you have to do is fight like only you can against your own self. Your own worst enemy is you."

"Careful there, uncle," I say socking him in the arm. "You're starting to sound like your mother."

"It's about time. Do whatever you have to do to get my Mama back home and soon, you hear?"

"You know I will." We hug tightly and then head our separate ways. I still get to see Mama on a regular basis but it must be devastating to everyone else who loves her to not know exactly what's up with our matriarch. As I pass by Esmeralda's house on my way to the bus stop I notice her animals staring me down. There time's about to come to an end, too. The sooner I crush that house the better.

It'll take me two buses to get to the coffee house for the study session, which will probably last a few hours. I wouldn't miss it for the world because Cameron's trifling ass is supposed to be there tonight and I'm ready to rip her apart for the games she's playing with Jeremy and me. Doesn't that trick know people get killed for that shit where I'm from?

"Christ feed the multitude with only one loaf of bread/Poor people there is something for you," Damian Marley sings through my cell. It's a call from Jeremy. I remember when he had his own ringtone. Now he's bundled in with the masses. Hopefully that'll change after tonight.

"Hey Lady J. Just wanted to warn you that the meeting's been moved to Cameron's house," Jeremy says. He knows that I'm rarely online unless it's absolutely necessary. "Same time, though."

"Thanks for letting me know," I say, settling in at the bus stop. Hopefully her clueless mother's not there.

"And Jayd," Jeremy says, pausing a moment too long.

"Yes, Jeremy?" I wave down the approaching bus.

"I'm sorry about how I reacted on Wednesday," Jeremy says, remorsefully.

"Me, too. But we can talk about it in an hour or so."

"The session starts in thirty minutes, Jayd. Is your car out of commission again?" he asks.

"Yes, but no worries. I'll be there with bells on."

I hang up my cell and secure it in my purse, ready for the long ride to Palos Verdes. Getting there is only half the battle: Walking up the steep hill her mega house is perched on will be my workout for the week. The last time we studied at Cameron's house I felt like a member of the staff, and her parents were watching my every move. This time will be no different, I'm sure.

By the time I arrive the study session is in full swing. I step into the large foyer where the housekeeper ushers me inside. There's plenty of food and drinks in the dining room, including coffee, green tea and a sandwich bar—all the makings for a long night in. when I enter the massive living area I notice Jeremy and Reid playing mental tennis with Othello's summary.

"Of course I believe in interracial dating, if that's what you want to call it," Jeremy says, casually. "It's a fact that we're all essentially African, therefore it's more accurate to say intercultural dating, if you will." I love the way Jeremy's mind works.

"No I won't, Jeremy," Reid says, boiling with generations of hate

182

between his family, and Jeremy's stirring the pot. Their brothers are all mortal enemies, ergo making them the worst of friends. "That's a preposterous theory and it's completely irrelevant when it comes to Shakespeare."

"Yeah, babe," Cameron says, pouring Jeremy more coffee. "I doubt that'll be on the test."

I attempt to discretely settle in on one of the oversized floor pillows but no such luck. Marcia spots me and signals for me to come sit next to her on one of the three couches in the room.

"Jayd, you made it," Jeremy says.

Cameron looks anything but pleased. "Jayd, so glad you got the update," she says, eyeing her soon to be ex fake boo. "Please help yourself to dinner."

"I did. And thank you, I will." I claim the spot next to Marcia who's way too excited for her first study session on the rich folks' side of town.

"OMG!" Marcia whispers excitedly into my right ear. "Jeremy looks just like Jerry Jerrod from Sex and the City. I so wish I was Samantha right now."

"Sit down, Marcia," I whisper back while making eye contact with the object of her desire. "He's mine."

"But I thought you broke up." I see she's caught up on some of the gossip circulating around Drama High.

"Not by choice," I say, retrieving my study materials from my backpack. "So again, sit down."

Marcia sees that I'm serious but can't let it go. "Samantha was stupid for walking away from all of that. Forget loving yourself. I'd love me some Jerrod forever if I had the chance."

"On to other themes in the work," Laura says, diverting the attention to herself and away from her man who's so obviously losing this battle with Jeremy. "Infidelity and trust issues in relationships."

I scan the study sheet and realize that we're only on the second out of ten topics. I say we stop debating and start researching. A sistah's definitely going to need a healthy snack to keep alert for this madness.

"Do you want anything?" I ask Marcia who shakes her head and points at her full plate.

I make my way into the dining area accessible through both the foyer and another hallway and claim a plate of my own. As I pick through the feast Jeremy and a couple of other classmates also make their way to the table.

"Jayd, we need to talk," Jeremy says, gently pulling my arm and leading me into the hallway. "This Keenan dude, is it serious?"

"Not that it's any of your business, but no. We're just friends," I say, snacking on a grape.

"Friends, huh. I remember when were friends and I stayed over your mom's house," Jeremy says, referring to the late night date he interrupted weeks ago. "I miss us, Jayd."

"Tell it to Cameron, Jeremy," I say, stepping away from him.

"She's blackmailing me, Jayd. You know this. Why can't we just be together in secret until this all blows over?"

I whip my head around and stare him down like Maman did Jean Paul in the spirit book when he came at her crazy, like this fool is doing to me. "There are two things wrong with that statement, Jeremy. Number one is that you act like the victim when in all actuality you got yourself into this mess and, as usual, you want me to help you shovel the crap, but I'm not having it this time around. I already busted her out in the principal's office on Friday, so the jig is up, Jeremy. And number two is that you take me for the type of girl who'd condone being a side chick when you should know better than to step to me with that bull. It's all or nothing."

Jeremy takes a step closer and kisses me hard, taking my balance and looming sense of revenge with it. He pulls away and forces me to look up into his eyes in an attempt to calm me down.

"Come on," he says, grabbing my hand and forcing me inside one of the bedrooms.

"Is this Cameron's room?" I ask, looking around the large, pink and white room. "Did she ever grow up?"

"Not really," he says, taking a deep breath. "But I don't want to talk about her. I want to talk about you and us, Jayd. It's been too long."

"I agree." I can't put my finger on it but something's off about this room. If I didn't know better I'd say that we were being watched.

"Okay, cool," Jeremy says, pulling me into his body by my waist. "Then you can tell that Keenan dude to bounce and I'll take you home tonight."

"Uhmm not so fast, sir," I say, backing away. "What about Cameron? Are you finally going to stand up to her for us?"

"Jayd, it's complicated," Jeremy says, reaching for me again but he can't touch me until he mans up. "You telling the principal is one thing. Cameron telling my parole officer is an entirely other set of circumstances that I don't want to deal with."

"I never took you for being spineless, Jeremy," I say, disappointed. I attempt to leave but he pulls me back and we fall onto the lushly made bed.

"Ouch!" Jeremy exclaims. "What the hell was that?"

185

He throws the multiple pillows off of the bed and reveals her hidden bag of tricks.

"I knew it!" This trick's been doing voodoo spells on Jeremy, and apparently on me and my grandmother, too. There's only one broad in town I know with these kinds of services for sale: Esmeralda. Esmeralda's reach knows no bounds, which is exactly why I can't do anything else until I stop this wench and her apprentice. Misty's become the school connect for Esmeralda's evil deeds. I understand needing a side hustle but this is ridiculous, even for my former friend.

"What the hell is all of this stuff?" Jeremy says, picking up an olive toned doll with curly, dark locs sewn into its head.

"Give me that," I say, taking it from him. "I've got to talk to Cameron."

"Wait a minute, Jayd," Jeremy says, blocking my advance. "We weren't even supposed to be in here. Just put it back and we can pretend like we never saw this stuff, whatever it is."

"This stuff is what's standing between me, you, and whole lot of other stuff you know nothing about." I stare at the two dolls resembling me and Mama and wish that I knew what to do with them—I'll have to leave that up to my elders. "It's one thing to go after me, Jeremy. I can take Cameron all day, any day if I so choose. But it's another thing entirely to go after my grandmother."

"I feel you, baby, but seriously. You're scaring me."

"You don't need to be afraid of me, Jeremy," I say, gathering the voodoo dolls, pin cushion and prepared tinctures to take back to Compton. It'll have to wait until morning because I know Dr. Whitmore has already put Mama back into a deep sleep for the night. We can't risk her being awake for too long. "You're not my enemy. Cameron is.

Misty is. Esmeralda and Mrs. Bennett are. They're the ones who need to fear me, Jeremy. Never you."

I would love to stay here with him but I can't afford to get off my game for a second. "I have to go." I head for the bedroom door with all of the diabolic tools in hand.

"What are you going to do?"

"Give them all a taste of their own medicines."

"Ever heard of a little thing called mercy?" Jeremy says, making light of my situation. If he only knew how real the danger is he wouldn't joke about such things.

"Yes, my Yeye invented it," I say, recalling an earlier odu about one of Oshune's older paths. "But this situation doesn't call for mercy. An eye for an eye is what my enemies believe in, and I'm about to make all of their wildest dreams come true."

"Well, what do we have here?" Cameron says, standing in my way. She looks down at the booty in my arms and snatches up my doll.

"Give it back, Cameron," I say, putting my hand out. "I don't want to hurt you." I dare the broad to try and stop me. With or without that doll Cameron's ass is mine.

"Bitch please," she says, sounding more like Mickey than the prissy white girl that she is. "You can't do anything to me. I've got you in the palm of my hand." Cameron lifts a pin out of the doll's shoulder and presses it into its left eye. "May your sight be unseen," Cameron says, looking dead at me.

"No!" I scream, dropping to my knees. All of the items fall to the ground. My vision fades to black rendering me helpless against my enemy, or so I think.

187

"Cameron, what are you doing?" Jeremy says, falling down beside me. "I don't believe this shit!"

"Jayd, hold on to your senses!" Maman screams into my head. *"Get in her head!"*

"But I can't see her," I say aloud. Cameron's laughing at her evil action and praising herself for doing so well. *"How can I get in her head without looking in her eyes? It defies everything I know about my mom's powers."*

"That's just it. You need to think outside the box, Jayd. You have more than your mother's sight at your disposal. Use the other powers to get where you need to be."

Blocking out Jeremy and Cameron's arguing, I focus on Cameron's voice, honing in on her high-pitched laugh. She sounds like she looks: A thin, teenaged heffa out to get me.

"Give me my doll." I rise to my feet and focus on her murky red aura. I can't make out her body but I can see the hatred emanating from her being—seeing the unseen is Queen Califia's gift and I am grateful for it.

"Never!" she raises another pin to the doll and goes for my heart.

Before Cameron can stab the mini me again, I slap her to the floor causing the doll to fly out of her hands. I jump on top of her and give this chick what she's been asking for.

"Jayd, stop! You're going to hurt her," Jeremy says, attempting to pull me off but now that my sight is back I'm not letting go.

"Get her off of me!" Cameron screams like she's afraid for her life.

"You want to play with dolls, Cameron? Then let's play." I take out a few strands of her hair by their roots and show them to her. "Our next play date's on me."

"Jayd, stop," Jeremy says, finally succeeding in rescuing his wench. "You are way out of line."

"Her? What about me?"

Jeremy looks from me to a seemingly wounded Cameron still on the floor in shock. "She never laid a hand on you, Jayd. What the hell is the matter with you?"

Several other students file into the hallway and see me standing over Cameron. Again, I'm deemed as the angry black girl who can't be invited anywhere. This must be how Mickey feels wherever she goes. It is in this moment that I realize I'll never truly fit into Jeremy's world.

"Nothing at all, Jeremy. I can see everything clearly now."

I make my way out of the crowded hall with all of Cameron's shit. I stuff it all in my backpack sitting on the living room floor next to a shocked Marcia and head for the front door. I've got bigger fish to fry. Mrs. Bennett's demands will have to wait.

"Never doubt yourself or your power."
-Mama
Drama High, volume 11: Cold As Ice

~ 18 ~
SIN PIEDAD

"Jayd, what's up girl? I'm just checking on you, making sure you got adequate transportation and shit," Chase says into my cell. I can tell he's trying to make me laugh but I'm not in the mood.

"I'm actually at the bus stop," I say, still hot from my recent encounter. I don't know what's worse, that Cameron nearly got the best of me or that Jeremy sided with her.

"Girl, please. I told you, I got you. Consider me your personal chauffeur until your whip is back in commission."

"Chase, I can't ask you to do that," I say, sitting on the covered clay bench. We're lucky if we have a sign to post up against while waiting for the bus in either of my hoods.

"You didn't ask, Jayd. I offered. Now, tell me where you are."

"Thanks for picking me up, Chase," I say, snapping the seatbelt locked. I had enough time to calm down and check my spirit notes for clues on how to dispose of Cameron and Esmeralda's toy collections. It seems that my recent visions about mirrors, water and rocks play into solving all of our problems. I need to confer with Mama about the exact plan but I know it involves burying these things for good.

"It's never a problem, Jayd," Chase says, lowering the music blaring through his state-of-the-art sound system. "Besides, Rancho Palos Verdes is my hood. Why didn't you call me earlier so I could come check for you?"

I can't believe Chase would drive damn near thirty miles on a

Saturday night to give me a ride. He's the most genuine friend I've ever had and probably the best dude that I know.

"Because you're not a taxi service, my brotha. Besides, you can't keep coming to my rescue."

Chase looks hurt by my words. "Whatever, Jayd. You know, for someone so outspoken most of the time you sure can be sheepish when it comes to asking for help, especially from someone who offers it with no limitations. So, Compton or Inglewood?"

"Honestly, I don't want to go home," I say, staring off into the distance. The ocean air is thick tonight and the full moon illuminates the sky.

"I'll take you anywhere you want to go."

"I need to hit up Big Sur for some jade stones," I say, recalling the burial incantation in my notes. "But I know that's out of the question."

"Well, Northern Cali is out but the stones aren't," he says, making a u-turn in the middle of Pacific Coast Highway. "There's a cave near one of our hangout spots with all kinds of sparkly stones in it. I bet you can find what you're looking for in there."

"I guess I was wrong," I say, relaxing a bit. "You are quite the knight in shining armor."

"You know it, my lady," Chase says, winking. He turns the melodic Outkast track back up as we cruise toward the ocean.

We park on Palos Verdes Drive and walk along the shore for a few minutes before reaching our destination.

"Down there," he says, pointing at a rocky area below the bluffs. "We have to do a little hiking but nothing you can't handle."

"Let's do it," I say, zipping my sweater. If I'd known I was going to be at the beach tonight I would've worn a thicker one. At least I wore sneakers, and Chase brought a couple of blankets just in case it gets too cold.

"I've got you, Jayd," Chase says, engulfing me in his Izzy Miyake scented sweater.

"What do you need these for anyway?" Chase asks, scanning the water for signs of colorful rocks. It took us some time to make it down here but I'm so glad that we did. I've never seen anything like this up close.

"I'm collecting the stones to bury some things my enemies created," I say, waiting for the tide to subside before scouring the water.

"That sounds like some deep shit right there," Chase says, walking several feet away from the tunnel and spreading the thick blankets on the small sandy area nearby. "Speaking of deep, what happened at the study session?"

"I don't want to go into everything, but Jeremy's an ass and Cameron can have him," I say, tossing a rock into the receding tide. "I know he's your boy and all but I'm through fighting for him."

"Jeremy and Rah are both cool with me, and Jeremy will always be the homie. But personally, I think that they're both complete imbeciles to let a queen like you slip away, especially that mark ass, bitch ass nigga Keenan—no offense."

"None taken," I say, genuinely smiling for the first time in hours. It's been a long time since someone had my back like Chase does.

"I'm going to light up," Chase says, sitting down on the blankets and pulling out a pack of cigarettes.

"I know it's tacky to tell you what to do, but seriously, you and

192

Alia need to cut that shit out," I say, removing my shoes and socks. The only way that I'm going to find what I need is to get my feet wet.

"Alia's no longer my concern," Chase says, switching the cigarettes for a half smoked blunt.

"What happened?" I step into the cold water and scan the rocks beneath the surface much like I did in one of my dreams. I turn my back to Chase as Maman's sight brightens the water and makes the jade stones easy to see. Chase was right: there's plenty of material here.

"Jealousy, like always. Sometimes I think relationships are pointless. I mean, you're friends in the beginning but the shackles lock into place and the friendship goes out the damned door."

"Why not just be friends with chicks instead of trying to wife them up all the time?" I ask, collecting multiple stones. These should be perfect for the ritual.

"Because friends don't come with benefits," he says, exhaling a large cloud of smoke in my direction.

"If they're your true friends, that's all the benefit you need." I place the stones in my pockets and keep hunting. It's better to have too many than too few. "Sex should be special, not some casual fling."

"And therein lies the problem with chicks," Chase says, completely faded. "Once the deed is done y'all go crazy. Why make a big a deal about the whole sex thing?"

"Because it is a big deal," I say, collecting the last of the stones. I can't carry any more.

"But it doesn't have to be. I mean, you could do it with a friend and get it over and done with. Losing your mind in love is optional, Jayd. I say control the circumstances, don't let them control you."

"Wise words, Mr. Carmichael," I say, making my way to the sand.

193

I don't know if it's the thick haze he's blowing that's sucking all of the oxygen out of the air or what, but my head's spinning. Chase catches me as I stumble down on the blanket next to him. I allow his nose to gently touch mine, accepting the thrust of his tongue as it makes its way between my lips.

"Chase, what are you doing?" I ask, coming up for air.

"What I've wanted to do since the first day I laid eyes on you in Drama class two years ago."

I look into his red eyes and remember that day and all of the days since then. If there's one brotha I can trust, it's him.

Before he can move in for round two I take control and return the affection.

"Okay," he says, giggling at my advance.

"What's so funny?" I retreat under the covers, embarrassed by my actions. What the hell was I thinking kissing Chase?

"I'm just saying," Chase says, joining me under the blanket. "I've been waiting for over two years to kiss you, and a peck's not going to do it." He pulls me into him; his eyes are wide open. His lips are so soft and his body, hard. I had no idea he would feel so right.

"Chase," I murmur between kisses. "Are we doing the right thing?"

"Do you want me to stop?"

I pause and consider his question. There are no other voices or visions in my head. There are no birds singing, but the stars are aligned and there is no fear in my heart, just like Netta said.

"No, I don't."

Chase smiles and continues kissing me until I'm completely covered by his strong body. He takes a condom out of his back pocket and places it into my hand. "Your choice, Jayd. It's all about you tonight."

Last night's still a slight blur to me. I don't feel any different but I know that I'm not virgin anymore, that's for sure. How we ended up back at Chase's house with his mom making us breakfast is also a mystery. But she's too happy that I'm here and I'm cool with the buffet.

"Good morning, baby. Jayd, how are you feeling, sweetie?" she says, pouring us fresh orange juice. We both sit at the kitchen island ready to dig in.

"I'm good," I say, taking a sip. "Tired, as usual."

"You have to take care of yourself, young lady. We need you around here," Mrs. Carmichael says, smiling big. She's always wanted me and her son together. "Chance, you should convince Jayd to stay here for the day and get some rest. I'm sure all of that back and forth to school must be exhausting, especially during your senior year."

"Jayd knows mi casa es her casa," Chase says, rubbing my thigh.

"Thanks, both of you but I've got to get back home," I say, allowing his hand to stay put. "I don't even want to think about all of the work I've got ahead of me today."

"Jayd, you should never argue with an attorney unless you're training to become one yourself," Mrs. Carmichael says. "I think you should consider staying here until your car is fixed. Chase told me you're having transportation challenges, and it's not like our house isn't big enough. We'd love to have you, and your grandmother knows you'd be in good hands."

I consider her offer, knowing that Nigel just moved out after a pleasant stay, and shake off the crazy idea. "I have hair clients in

195

Inglewood and I have to work in Compton during the week."

"Jayd, think about it. I'm sure it can all be worked out."

"I think it's a swell idea," Chase says, backing his mom.

I feel like I'm being ambushed.

"Chance, don't forget to make an appointment for your deposition with your father's attorney next week. I want this divorce done with by the end of the month."

"Sure thing, mom," Chase says, piling his plate with bacon and eggs.

Mrs. Carmichael's cell rings. "This is Lindsay." After few moments of silence she yells into her phone. Someone's got her hotter than fish grease early on a Sunday morning.

"Hell no David can't have the villas in Cancun, Italy or anywhere else for that matter. Excuse me you two," Mrs. Carmichael says, stepping out of the kitchen. "Chance, see that Jayd gets enough to eat."

"I love how she still calls you Chance," I say, eating off of his plate. He's got enough for both us.

"My mom named me after the main character in Sweet Bird of Youth. She loved that movie and Paul Newman."

"Never heard of it," I say, adding toast to the collection.

"You should check it out some time. Then you'll see that I didn't have much of a choice in how I turned out."

"Yeah, but your birth name is Chase, remember?"

"Chase, Chance…what's in a name, really?" Chase says.

The doorbell rings. Chase leaves me alone to answer it. If he takes too long he's going to be one hungry brotha when he returns.

"Jayd, I want you to meet some friends of mine," Chase says, stepping back into the kitchen. "Javier and Mauricio, this is Jayd, the

196

sistah I was telling y'all about."

"Senorita Jayd, it's a pleasure to finally meet you," Javier says, kissing the back of my hand.

"Likewise, but I haven't heard anything about you two."

"That's because you weren't supposed to until it was the right time. I believe you know our hermanita, Maggie," Mauricio says, making the link.

"Chase is our newest investor," Javier says, taking a seat at the kitchen table near the window. "And Maggie says you and she go way back, like family."

"Si, la familia," Mauricio says, nodding affirmatively. "She told us you're having problems with Esmeralda's house, no?"

I look at Chase who's posted by the entrance and wonder what the hell is really going on. "I'm not sure what you've heard but the issues I've got with Esmeralda are personal, not street."

"Chase, filled us in on tu problemas," Javier says. "Sin piedad is our family name, and also the name of our family's Santeria house. Hector's been our adversary for many years, and now that he's working with Esmeralda, he's become a serious thorn in mi abuelita's side."

"Si, and we're also against that man made shit Esmeralda's slanging through that punk, G," Mauricio says, letting all of his cards out on the table. "From where I'm sitting, we're family, Jayd. We have the same enemies, and I think we can be of a great help to one another."

"Si, Jayd. Sin piedad means no mercy. Whatever we do, we do with the full understanding that our adversary deserves no mercy from us because of the simple fact that he or she is our enemy," Javier says. "So, like I said, having the same enemies makes us family in my book."

"And how do you play into all of this, Chase?" I ask, seeing my friend through new eyes. He's known more about me and my family than he's ever let on. His mother and Mama go way back but I didn't think she shared it with Chase. I guess now that our worlds are crossing he's ready to step in and be the friend that I need on my side to win this battle.

"You remember when we saw the movie Savages?" Chase says, folding his arms across his chest. "Well, I'm that dude who believes weed makes the world a better place. The fact that we have to go through illegal means to keep the peace isn't my fault, nor is it my concern. I just want you to be happy and safe again, Jayd."

I look at Chase, Javier and Mauricio and realize that we're all on the same side. They're my street and spirit soldiers, and like any embattled queen, I need an army to go to war.

"Sin piedad," Mauricio says, raising his glass of juice in the air like it's spiked.

"Sin piedad," Javier and Chase say, also raising their glasses.

I pick up my glass of water and catch my reflection seeing myself as the young woman I feel like I am. "Sin piedad," I say, joining the salute. "The time for playing childish games is over. Let's put an end to Esmeralda's reign once and for all."

"That a girl," Chase says, walking over and kissing me on the forehead. "Whatever you need me to do, I'm here."

"I know, Chase. Believe me, I know."

EPILOGUE

Practicing what I've learned over the past couple of weeks, I purposefully fell into a deep sleep tonight thinking about how to declare a private war on Esmeralda's house without my grandmother and mother finding out. I have been in and out of a dream state ever since. I can feel the answer slowly revealing itself.

"If you don't want us to see, then take us off of your arm," Queen Califia says, looking down at my jade bracelets. "They represent the five of us because we are your jotos—your sponsoring elders. Maman is your ancestral joto who came with you into this realm. She cannot be removed. But if at any time you don't want the rest of us to see what you see, remove a single bracelet and call one of our names at the same time. We won't be able to hear a thing you think or witness a vision you have."

"Is that all I have to do?" I follow my ancestor's directions and feel the mental separation. Where there were five bracelets there are now only three.

"Place them inside of your Oshune vessel for safe keeping," Queen Califia says, removing the thick cloth cover. "Like the voodoo dolls, these possess ashe, too."

I gently set the fragile jewelry down in the water with the stones and other sacred items that represent our mother orisha. "If I had known it was that easy I would've done this a long time ago."

Queen Califia replaces the cover and smiles. "Sometimes the simplest answer is the most difficult one to see, iyawo."

I wake up and shake my head at the powerful vision. My left arm is noticeably lighter without the extra weight.

"You good, Jayd?" Chase asks, reaching out for my hand.

"Yes, I'm perfect." I pat his hand and turn back over to finish my night's sleep. Sometimes my dreams are so active that they prevent a completely restful slumber. Still, I wouldn't trade this spirit talk for anything in the world.

Discussion Questions

1. Does Nigel have the right to sue for permanent custody of Nickey? How will he make a better home for Mickey's daughter?

2. Do you think Jayd can handle a sexual relationship? Why or why not?

3. Was Mama right to make Dr. Whitmore her medical proxy instead of her husband? Explain your thoughts.

4. Make a pros and cons list of all of the reasons Jayd should/shouldn't allow Rah to stay in her life as a friend.

5. Describe a time when you felt trapped between two friends or situations where you had to make a difficult choice. What did you do?

6. Have you ever had a lucid dream that came true in reality? If so, please describe. If not, would you like to have this experience? Why or why not?

7. Explain how you think Jayd's naturally brown eyes influence her powers.

Stay tuned for the next book
in the DRAMA HIGH series,
SWEET DREAMS

RECOMMENDED READING

Listed below are a few of my favorite writers. The list is in no particular order and always changing. Please feel free to send me your favorites at **www.DramaHigh.com.**

OCTAVIA E. BUTLER

ALICE WALKER

ZORA NEALE HURSTON

TINA MCELROY ANSA

JAMES BALDWIN

MARYSE CONDE

MADISON SMART BELL

R.M. JOHNSON

NAPOLEON HILL

JACKIE COLLINS

MARY HIGGINS CLARK

J.K. ROWLING

STEPHEN KING

IYANLA VANZANT

RHONDA BYRNE

AMY TAN

NATHAN MCCALL

NIKKI GIOVANNI

EDWIDGE DANTICAT

J. CALIFORNIA COOPER

TONI CADE BAMBARA

RICHARD WRIGHT

GLORIA NAYLOR

JAMES PATTERSON

LUISAH TEISH

QUEEN AFUA

BRI. MAYA TIWARI

HILL HARPER

JOSEPH CAMPBELL

TANANARIVE DUE

ANNE RICE

L.A. BANKS

FRANCINE PASCAL

SANDRA CISNEROS

DANIELLE STEELE

CAROLYN RODGERS

STEPHANIE ROSE BIRD

CHIEF FAMA

GWENDOLYN BROOKS

BELL HOOKS

AMIRI BARAKA

START YOUR OWN BOOK CLUB

Courtesy of the DRAMA HIGH series

ABOUT THIS GUIDE

The following is intended to help you get the Book Club you've always
wanted up and running! Enjoy!

Start Your Own Book Club

A Book Club is not only a great way to make friends, but is also a fun and safe environment for you to express your views and opinions on everything from fashion to teen pregnancy? A Teen Book Club can also become a forum or venue to air grievances and plan remedies for problems.

The People
To start, all you need is yourself and at least one other person. There's no criteria for who this person or persons should be other than a desire to read and a commitment to read and discuss during a certain time frame.

The Rules
Just like in Jayd's life, sometimes even Book Club discussions can be filled with much drama. People tend to disagree with each other, cut each other off when speaking, and take criticism personally. So, there should be some ground rules:

1. Do not attack people for their ideas or opinions.
2. When you disagree with a book club member on a point, disagree respectfully. This means that you do not denigrate another person for their ideas or even their ideas, themselves i.e. no name calling or saying, "That's stupid!" Instead, say, "I can respect your position, however, I feel differently."
3. Back up your opinions with concrete evidence, either from the book in question or life in general.
4. Allow every one a turn to comment.
5. Do not cut a member off when they are speaking. Respectfully, wait your turn.
6. Critique only the idea (and do so responsibly; again, saying simply, "That's stupid!" is not allowed). Do not critique the person.
7. Every member must agree to and abide by the ground rules.

*Feel free to add any other ground rules you think might be necessary.

The Meeting Place
Once you've decided on members, and agreed to the ground rules, you should decide on a place to meet. This could be the local library, the school library, your favorite restaurant, a bookstore, or a member's home. Remember, though, if you decide to hold your sessions at a member's home, the location should rotate to another member's home for the next sessions. It's also polite for guests to bring treats when attending a Book Club meeting at a member's home. If you choose to hold your meetings in a public place, always remember to ask the permission of the librarian or store manager. If you decide to hold your meetings in a local bookstore, ask the manager to post a flyer in the window announcing the Book Club to attract more members if you so desire.

Timing is Everything
Teenagers of today are all much busier than teenagers of the past. You're probably thinking, "Between Chorus Rehearsals, the Drama Club, and oh yeah, my job, when will I ever have time to read another book that doesn't feature Romeo and Juliet!" Well, there's always time, if it's time well-planned and time planned ahead. You and your Book Club can decide to meet as often or as little as is appropriate for your bustling schedules. **Once a month** is a favorite option. **Sleepover Book Club** meetings—if you're open to excluding one gender—is also a favorite option. And in this day of high-tech, savvy teens, **Internet Discussion Groups** are also an appealing option. Just choose what's right for you!

Well, you've got the people, the ground rules, the place, and the time. All you need now is a book!

The Book
Choosing a book is the most fun. NO MERCY is of course an excellent choice, and since it's a series, you won't soon run out of books to read and discuss. Your Book Club can also have comparative discussions as you compare the first book, THE FIGHT, to the second, SECOND CHANCE, and so on.

But depending on your reading appetite, you may want to veer outside of the DRAMA HIGH series. That's okay. There are plenty of options available.

Don't be afraid to mix it up. Nonfiction is just as good as fiction, and a fun way to learn about from whence we came without the monotony of a history book. Science Fiction and Fantasy can be fun too!

And always, always, research the author. You may find the author has a website where you can post your Book Club's questions or comments. The author may even have an email address available so you can correspond directly. Authors will also sit in on your Book Club, either in person, or on the phone, and this can be a fun way to discuss the boo as well!

The Discussion

Every good Book Club discussion starts with questions. **NO MERCY,** as well as every other book in the **DRAMA HIGH** series comes along with a Reading Group Guide for your convenience, though of course, it's fine to make up your own. Here are some sample questions to get started:

1. What's this book all about anyway?
2. Who are the characters? Do we like them? Do they remind us of real people?
3. Was the story interesting? Were real issues of concern to you examined?
4. Were there details that didn't quite work for you or ring true?
5. Did the author create a believable environment—one that you can visualize?
6. Was the ending satisfying?
7. Would you read another book from this author?

Record Keeper

It's generally a good idea to have someone keep track of the books you read. Often libraries and schools will hold reading drives where you're rewarded for having read a certain number of books in a certain time period. Perhaps, a pizza party awaits!

Get Your Teachers and Parents Involved

Teachers and Parents love it when kids get together and read. So involve your teachers and parents. Your Book Club may read a particular book where it would help to have an adult's perspective as part of the discussion. Teachers may also be able to include what you're doing as a Book Club in the classroom curriculum. That way books you love to read like DRAMA HIGH can find a place in your classroom alongside of the books you don't love to read so much.

CPSIA information can be obtained at www.ICGtesting.com
Printed in the USA
LVOW05s0656280914

406195LV00004B/25/P